THE VEGAS BILLIONAIRE

AN INTERNATIONAL BILLIONAIRE CLUB SERIES

BRITNEY M MILLS

CRYSTAL CANYON PRESS

*W*alking out of the large gym on the lower floor of his resort hotel, Evan Pearson wiped his forehead with a towel and walked toward the smoothie counter. With the remodel of several large rooms on the ground floor, he had more fires to put out than normal. The fact that he'd had to run some of the tension off during lunch wasn't a good sign of how the day was going, and he could feel the beginnings of a headache just behind his eyes.

"The usual, Cory," he said, dropping onto a stool next to the counter.

The lanky college kid behind the counter nodded and pulled out several ingredients, pouring them into the large blender.

A lot of people had balked at the idea of a section dedicated to smoothies and flavored drinks, wondering if would be worth it in his large hotel, but it was one of the highest earning stores throughout his resort.

"How are things today, Mr. Pearson?" Cory asked over the sound of the blender.

Wiping his face once more with his towel, Evan said,

"Another day at the office. How goes college? You're a business major, right?"

The young man nodded and smiled. "It's harder than I thought it would be."

Grinning, Evan nodded, remembering his time as a student at Hawthorne. It had been seven years since graduation, but he could still remember a lot of his teachers and their advice through the four years he'd been there. "If you ever need help with it, or choosing a future career, come see me. I had some great people help me out in my life, and I like to return the favor."

His mind turned to Dan Montgomery, one of the coaches of the football team and house mentor to his fraternity, Delta Phi. The wisdom Dan had shared throughout their relationship was beyond his years, and Evan would always be grateful for it. Since Coach's passing at the beginning of the year, Evan had thought about him even more, grateful to have Dan's voice in his head.

"I'd love that, sir. Business is so broad, and any help I can get to whittle it down would be great." Cory grinned, and his comment made Evan throw back his head and laugh.

Cory handed the Styrofoam cup filled with a chocolate protein smoothie and a straw across the counter and nodded, looking over Evan's shoulder at a woman who'd just walked in. "What can I get you?"

"Can I get a strawberry smoothie with a shot of protein?" The woman's voice was familiar, and Evan spun to look back.

"Taryn?"

She turned, flashing him a smile. "Hey, little brother. Your manager, Brent, told me I'd find you here."

"Put it on my account, Cory." Evan took a sip of his smoothie as he waited for her order to be ready.

"You don't have to do that," she said, grinning at him. She

was older than him by two years, but he'd always been taught to take care of his sisters, no matter what stage of life he was in.

She walked over to stand by him and grinned.

"What brings you to Vegas? I thought you were back in California, planning your wedding."

Taryn whipped her long ponytail around and rolled her eyes. "I'm here for FitCon. It starts tomorrow, but I thought I'd stop by and say hi before I get checked into my hotel."

Raising his eyebrows, he asked, "Why aren't you staying here? You could for free, you know."

With a cheesy grin, Taryn said, "I know, but this was just easier because then I don't have to go further than across the street from the convention center to the hotel. After these long days, it will be hard enough to make it to my room before I fall asleep."

Taryn had become a health-and-fitness nut a few years before and worked to share tips and tricks on getting or staying healthy with her followers on Quickstagram, the app Evan's triplet brother, Aiden, had designed.

"How's Travis? Is he almost done with his rotations?" Evan took another sip and waited for the answer as Taryn moved to grab her smoothie and rejoin him.

"He's really good. I'll fly back to California at the end of the week, and he'll be back then for a few weeks before the wedding. Speaking of," she said, jutting out her bottom lip and giving him sad eyes. "I need to ask you a favor."

"Okay." Evan felt his stomach clench as he waited for her question. Taryn always asked some of the hardest questions, and he hoped it wouldn't be dangerous this time.

She took a long sip of her smoothie, and he felt his irritation rise. It had to be something big for her to wait this long. Turning, she moved to sit down at a table.

When he slid into the chair opposite her, she asked,

"Would you mind if we use the convention room for our wedding?"

Frowning, Evan said, "What about the 'amazing place' you had booked in California? I thought that was all set."

She bit her upper lip, and he could see the emotion playing in her eyes. When she spoke, her voice sounded a bit wobbly, as if she could break into tears at any moment. "Our wedding planner skipped town with our deposit and all the extra money we'd put toward the rentals. We've filed all the paperwork to get it back, but if they can't find her, it will be no use. She never booked the venue, caterers, or anything, so I'm here, stuck at square one, trying to get things figured out on a smaller budget. My wedding is in six weeks, and I'm kind of freaking out a bit."

"You're still getting married before Thanksgiving?" he asked.

When she nodded, he said, "I'm not sure it will be completely done by then. I've been working on that remodel for a few months, and they're just barely getting all the finish work for it."

"Six weeks will be enough time. All you need to do is paint, right?"

Evan shook his head. Only his sister would think it was as easy as just snapping his fingers to get things done. With all of the work in the connecting rooms, it could take over a month to paint the entire section, and as it was, he needed to find a painter. His previous one had moved to Arizona to be closer to his wife's parents, and Evan had struggled to find someone consistent enough to do the job.

"I'll see what I can do. If it's not done, we'll just have it in the courtyard. I'm sure the fountain would look great in your pictures."

Taryn pushed his shoulder and frowned. "In November? I know this is Vegas, but it's still colder in the fall. Just promise me you'll try to get the room done? It will help us so much to have things figured out."

"Are you doing all the planning yourself now?"

She shook her head. "No, I've asked Sadie Gibson to help. She's a wedding planner, and Aubrey vouched for her skills. She was featured in one of the wedding magazines a few months back, so I'd say I'm in good hands. I just wish I'd known that from the start."

Evan tried to picture the red-headed girl who'd been attached at the hip with his triplet sister since they were young. She'd gone to high school with Evan, Aubrey, and Aiden, and had been around for many of the same parties. What would she be like now?

Sadie and Aubrey had been roommates since college, but it had been some time since he'd seen her. Graduation from Hawthorne was probably the last. She'd always been nice, but he'd been the big-shot football player and had moved in different circles throughout college. Not much time to remember one of his hometown girls.

"Is that what Sadie does now? Plan weddings?" Evan looked at Taryn for confirmation.

"She's a pretty famous planner. But you've avoided everything about weddings for the past five years, so I can understand why you wouldn't know that."

Evan licked his lips, trying to get rid of the sudden dryness at the turn of the conversation. Taryn's bluntness at his avoidance of weddings caused bile to rise in his throat. He'd finally gotten over being left at the altar, but each time July 23rd rolled around, he did everything he could to possibly forget about the memories from that day.

The experience had soured him from even dating, knowing he'd eventually want something more than being a boyfriend and not trusting he wouldn't be abandoned again. He couldn't put himself through that again. Marriage was something he'd always wanted, but now it just gave him nightmares.

Taryn shifted her purse on her arm. "She just got done with Maleah Strong's wedding two weeks ago, and it was a vision. I only hope she can do something like that for our wedding." She took another sip of her drink and looked up at him. "What about your dating life? Have you been out with anyone lately?"

The casual question held so much behind it. When was the last time he'd even gone on a date? The last one he could remember was someone Taryn had tried to line him up with, and she'd been more interested in feeling his biceps than an actual conversation.

"You do know I work an insane amount of hours a week and then have to travel often to check on my other hotels. I'm not sure any woman would appreciate a relationship like that."

"I know it still hurts, Evan, but Stacey leaving you at the altar shouldn't be the end of your dating life. You need to get out there and keep trying. You'll find someone."

If only it were that easy. He'd thought he and Stacey would be together, happily, for the rest of forever. He'd proposed because he thought he couldn't live without her after all the years growing up together. But she'd turned around and married one of his good friends from high school, driving the knife in even further.

Evan threw back his head and laughed, trying to think of a way to switch the direction of their conversation. "Right, because running resort hotels is a side job. I just need to get through these remodels with my sanity, and then maybe I'll think about dating. But don't think since you'll be happily married that you can set me up over and over with every girl you find out is single."

Feigning hurt, Taryn said, "I'm the best matchmaker there is. You're just too picky."

"No, Taryn, you're the best fitness blogger I've ever seen, but Cupid you are not."

Scrunching her nose, she pulled her purse over her shoulder. "Just wait. I'll make sure you find someone amazing, and she'll make sure to put you in your place, Mr. Billionaire." She winked. "I have to head over. I'm supposed to help set up the registration table."

They stood, and she leaned in to give him a hug. "You'll be fine, Ev. Just don't close yourself off completely to love."

When they pulled apart, Evan said, "Tell Travis hi for me."

Taryn nodded and disappeared through the door.

Evan walked over to the elevator. When it opened, he pushed the button for the penthouse and swiped his card to allow the elevator to grant the request. Leaning back against the wall of the elevator, Evan knew he needed to make a few calls and get things lined up to make his sister's new wedding dreams come true.

If love was going to happen in his life, it would have to be spontaneous, because he wasn't up for any more blind dates. Even as he thought it, the loneliness gnawed at his chest. Doing his best to push it away, he stepped out of the elevator and walked to the master suite. With his emotions running high, he just needed something to calm him down before he was needed at his afternoon meeting. He just hoped a hot shower would do the trick.

CHAPTER 2

*S*adie sifted through the towering pile of papers and samples on her large desk. Right now she wished she had an office, and a full-time assistant. She'd thought about finding an office space a few months ago, to help her with the clutter and to leave some of her work behind at the office when she went home. But with the schedule she kept and the actual amount of time she was home, it wasn't worth it to rent out anything else.

Pulling up the Quickstagram app, Sadie thought about Aiden Pearson, the creator and one of her childhood friends. That usually led to thoughts of Evan, Aiden's triplet brother, and the ridiculous crush she'd had on him since they were young. As much as she wanted to forget the arrogant jerk, her brain and heart couldn't seem to agree on that, and she had to focus on other things in order to not feel like a lame schoolgirl still dreaming about the guy she could never have.

It only took a few minutes to post several of the edited photos the photographer had sent her from her most recent planning success, the wedding of Maleah Strong, the pop singer. She'd chosen the Four Seasons in New York City as the venue, and it had been one of Sadie's favorite weddings to date. The different elements within the classy silver-and-gold theme had come together perfectly, even after the constant internal debate Sadie'd had up to the day before the wedding.

Maleah had been easy to work with, as she had some idea of what she wanted and then let Sadie try out some things instead of breathing down her neck, like some past brides had. Maybe it was because she was refining her business and clarifying her role that the last few weddings she'd put together were easier in that respect.

After arriving back in LA, Sadie hadn't really had time to get used to the time change again before she'd come to the aid of her best friend's sister. She'd heard about cases where the wedding planner walked away from the job without doing a thing, and it baffled her how someone could do that. Then again, everyone had their quirks.

Taryn had called a few days ago, pleading, and although the schedule would be tight, Sadie had agreed. With another wedding to plan for in December, she'd be doing double duty for a few weeks, but she didn't want to turn down work, especially now that all of her hard work was paying off.

From what it sounded like, the wedding would be taking place at Evan's resort hotel in Las Vegas, which would mean she'd have to see him again. The thought of it sent a chill running through her. She'd always been the bookish nerd with thick coke-bottle glasses, her hair never cooperating. She looked into the mirror, smoothing it with a sigh. Thank goodness the years had helped things settle down, and the color wasn't quite the orange it had once been.

With contacts to reveal more of her emerald-green eyes, she wondered what Evan would think when he saw her. Or would he even recognize her? She wasn't sure which one she preferred, but she felt the knots already beginning to form as she thought about it.

She looked back down at the table, knowing she was going to have to get her feelings under control. The last few times she'd seen him, he'd been cruel to her and a lot of others, and yet she still hung on in the hopes that there was something underneath his prickly exterior.

Sadie's phone vibrated on the table, and she had to move several things to discover where it had gone. The number was from California, and she paused, trying to remember if she'd seen the number before. She'd had to change her phone number the year before after getting several stalker-like phone calls, but she still felt those same nerves and allowed the call to go to voicemail. She almost forgot about it until the beep sounded almost three minutes later, the notification popping up on her locked screen.

Listening to the voicemail, she almost fell off her chair.

"Hi, Sadie, this is Charleigh French, the actress." The woman paused for a moment and then said, "My fiancé and I heard about you from Maleah's wedding. We would love to see some of your work on another wedding before we settle on a wedding planner, and you are the gal to talk to according to all of our references. Jackie Cooper told me she loved the experience of working with you two years ago on her wedding. Anyway, give me a call when you get this."

Sadie grabbed a pen and scribbled down the number Charleigh left before hanging up.

Sadie held the phone away from her ear, looking at the screen but not really seeing it. Charleigh French was the up-and-coming movie star, having starred in three box office hits since the beginning of the year. Now the question was when Sadie should call her back. Was it too soon to call back now? Or should she wait several hours to look like she was extremely busy?

After debating for several moments, she dialed the number Charleigh gave her and took shallow breaths, hoping to calm the explosion of emotions.

"Hello?" Charleigh answered.

Sadie panicked, pressing her palm against her forehead. "Um, hi. This is Sadie Gibson. I just received a call and was told to call back at this number?" She hoped the question at the end wasn't terribly noticeable. She wanted to sound like a confident professional, but instead, it sounded like she was fangirling.

"Sadie. Thanks for getting back to me so quickly. This is Charleigh."

"Oh good. I was worried I'd dialed the wrong number or something."

A light chuckle carried through the phone, and the woman said, "Okay, so you already got my message. Do you have any weddings we can stop by and see in the next few weeks?"

"Actually, I'm working on one that will be the week of Thanksgiving. Is there a certain theme or style you prefer?"

Seconds ticked by, and Sadie wondered if the call had been dropped, when Charleigh said, "I guess all the classic things. White dress, black tux, color in touches throughout the display. White roses and plenty of bling."

Sadie looked over the items on the table and realized that everything she'd planned for Taryn's wedding so far was completely opposite of that: rustic, homey, with touches of bling here and there.

"Okay, that will give me an idea. When are you planning to have your wedding?"

"We were thinking in Monaco in June. But that's hush-hush. We're trying to make it small so the word doesn't get out. I'd prefer not to have several strangers with cameras arrive, you know?"

Sadie grinned. It was a concern Maleah had expressed as well. "I completely understand. Okay, I will send you the details of the November wedding, and then we'll go from there."

"Sounds good. I'll send you an address for where to send an invitation so we can attend, if that's okay with the bride and groom, of course. I'm hoping to get some inspiration as I haven't done a thing to start planning the wedding."

Sadie's brain was blank, as if it had stopped working at the idea of talking to a movie star. Words finally started ticking through her brain, and she said, "If you'd like a few other wedding themes I've done, I can email them to you. One of the weddings I did was also featured in the *All Things Wedding* magazine two months ago, and that wedding sounds similar to what you're looking for. My biggest suggestion is to start a board of your likes and dislikes on ClipBoard. That will be the easiest way for me to get a feel for your taste, and there are so many great ideas people have clipped on there."

They finished the conversation, and Sadie sat back, stunned. She'd never thought she'd have the opportunity to plan weddings for celebrities, but as her reputation kept growing, the opportunities continued to increase as well.

Pulling out her calendar, Sadie made a few adjustments to the schedule. The wedding for the Montgomerys was going to be held two days before Christmas in Aspen. She was grateful that most of the big stuff had been decided on and ordered, meaning there would only be small things Sadie would need to check on here and there. After Taryn's wedding, she would go back to it in full force, but for now, she could focus on a Vegas wedding.

Leaning forward, she knew she was going to have to get Taryn's wedding perfect. Being the wedding coordinator for

Charleigh French's wedding would be the gig of a lifetime and could make her earnings skyrocket. The only problem was impressing Charleigh with what Taryn had requested. She might have to add persuasion to her list of things to get done.

CHAPTER 3

The captain of the plane asked for seat belts to be buckled as they made their descent into Las Vegas. Sadie was grateful Aubrey had decided to fly out with her even though it was only for a weekend. She would be driving to visit her family in Aspen Hollow, Utah, the following Monday.

As they found Sadie's large suitcase in the baggage claim area, Aubrey said, "Are you ready for this?"

Sadie grinned. "Yep. I feel really good about my plan and schedule so far. Sure, there will be a lot of things that have to line up perfectly in the next five weeks, but I think with my ideas and your brother's connections, we might be able to pull it off."

"Yeah, Evan definitely knows a lot of people. That comes in handy more often than I care to admit." Aubrey laughed, her dark hair cascading down her back.

As her insides turned at the mention of his name, Sadie tried to push away the curiosity about Evan stirring inside her. She'd always tried to keep the conversation casual when it came to him, hoping not to tip off her best friend that she liked her brother, even after years had passed. Maybe seeing him again would help her get over him this time.

"Oh really? When have you used his connections?" Sadie turned to her best friend and narrowed her eyes, scrutinizing her face.

Aubrey shrugged. "Well, I haven't really done that, but I know many people who have. Sometimes I feel bad for Evan and Aiden. A lot of people cling to them because they have money."

Sadie smiled, remembering the time when Aubrey's triplet siblings had started seeing a lot of success in their fields. Aubrey had questioned whether or not nursing was something she should continue. She'd always loved nursing, but it was surprising how some people didn't value that as much because she didn't have billions in her bank account. Some even thought of her as a failure because she wasn't as "successful" as the other two. When she'd come to terms with the fact that nursing was noble and that no one expected her to do something she didn't want to do, her life changed, and Sadie could see the peace that had finally rested over her.

"We're there to put them in their place, though, right?" Sadie smirked.

Aubrey threw her head back and laughed. "Of course. But for now, let's take advantage of our mini vacation and enjoy the weekend."

Sadie pushed Aubrey's shoulder, causing her to stumble to the side a few steps. "Vacation for you. I'll be working the entire time."

Aubrey giggled and moved back next to Sadie, motioning to the line of guys waiting with names written on papers or tablets. An older gentleman with salt-and-pepper hair held a sign with their names.

Sadie pointed to the tablet. "That's us."

"Hi, George." Aubrey dropped her bags and went on tiptoe to hug the large man.

They pulled apart, and the man grinned. "It's a pleasure to see you again, Miss Pearson. It's been too long."

"That it has. How are Holly and the kids?"

"Doing well, miss. Thank you for asking. Let me get your bags. The car is out this way." George reached forward, taking the handles of the suitcases from the girls and moving toward the wall of windows to the outdoors.

As they walked outside, Sadie was grateful it wasn't sweltering at the beginning of October. Leaning over to Aubrey, she gestured to the man walking in front of them and asked, "How do you know him?"

"Evan hired George when he bought his first hotel in Las Vegas. He's kind of like part of the family. He even brought his family to dinner at my parents' house once. You know, one of those times when I invited you to come hang out at a family party and you turned me down."

"That's what a boyfriend is for," Sadie said, flashing Aubrey a mischievous grin. "Besides, the longer I can stay away from Aspen Hollow, the better."

George opened the door of a white limo, and Sadie slid in after Aubrey, hearing the click of the door as he closed it.

"Your parents don't live there anymore, so why don't you like it?" Aubrey turned her hazel eyes toward her. This was when Sadie wished her friend wasn't so inquisitive.

"All I think about are the bad memories from that place. It's just better if I don't have to relive that again. How's Lance? I feel like I haven't been able to talk to you since I've been in New York."

Aubrey grimaced. "We decided to go our separate ways. He didn't like the fact that I was working extra shifts to be able to go see my parents. If he really knew me, he'd know I love decorating for the fall festival. I wait all year just so I can get things ready for it."

"That and Christmas." Sadie reached over and patted her friend's hand. "I'm sorry, girl. You'll find someone soon."

"You will too. Maybe this wedding will bring out all the good-looking normal guys and we can both benefit."

Sadie laughed and nodded, feeling a small hollow space in her chest. There wouldn't be a guy who could take the fear of marriage out of her. But she could hope that for her friend.

* * *

THE RIDE to the resort was quick, the driver navigating the roads with experience and efficiency. Evan's assistant checked Sadie and Aubrey into one of the upper suites, and upon walking into it, Sadie couldn't close her mouth. It seemed like an exorbitant amount of money was spent on the furnishings and the look, and in Sadie's opinion, they'd done a great job.

"Are you sure Evan doesn't need to rent this room out? It seems like this should be going for quite a bit." Had he personally arranged for them to stay in such a big space? Or was this just the standard Pearson-family accommodation?

Aubrey waved it off. "He'll be fine. There are probably three thousand rooms in this complex. With all the shopping below and the shows that come to town, he'll be fine without this room for a few weeks."

"I'm not staying in this room the entire time, or I better not be. I might get too used to it and then never be happy in our small apartment."

"You can enjoy things and then find a way to get back to normal. Besides, you don't stay long at our apartment anyway."

Biting her bottom lip, Sadie said, "True."

"Do you think you'll be a wedding planner forever? I mean, it seems like a great adventure, jet-setting around the world for each event, but what happens when you get married and have a family?" Aubrey's face was neutral, and Sadie knew she was just asking, like she did almost every six months.

Flopping onto the bed, Sadie stared at the ceiling. "I love this, Aub. It's like fulfilling every dream I could have to get married. I love kids; I just don't know if a family is in the cards for me."

"Just because your parents' divorce was less than civil doesn't mean that relationship problems are genetic. You're beautiful, and I would kill for your auburn hair. Besides, you're sweet, funny, and you genuinely care about people. Some guy would be hitting the jackpot if he landed you."

"What about you?" Sadie asked, sitting up and glaring at her friend. "We're only a month apart. Why do I have to be dating someone if you aren't either?"

"Because I worry about you. You used to have dreams about your wedding, planning every detail, right down to the cream puffs. It's been nine years, Sadie. Your parents are better off now, don't you think?"

Nodding, Sadie had to agree. It had been hard to accept new spouses for her parents, and although they still bickered when they were together, she was grateful things weren't as bad as they'd been at the beginning. It was a wonder they'd each wanted to marry again after the year in court and several restraining orders.

She needed a break from the conversation. "I'm going to fill the ice bucket. I feel like my tongue has turned into sandpaper after the flight." Sadie lifted the bucket from near the sink and moved toward the door.

"Just use the water in the mini fridge."

Feeling the need for air, Sadie shook her head. "No, I think I'd drain it right now. I'll be right back."

Ducking into the hall before Aubrey could come up with another excuse, Sadie breathed a sigh of relief that she'd been able to escape the room. She loved Aubrey like an actual sister, more than her own, actually, but there were times when she just needed a break to think things through on her own, without Aubrey trying to solve everything for her.

Reading the sign on the wall pointing the direction to the ice machine, she walked to the left, admiring the wood trim of the hallway. Evan, or more probably his designer, had good taste in finish work and décor, pulling all the pieces together.

She'd been looking up at the lights as she walked when she bumped into something hard, causing her to take a step back. At first she thought it was the wall, but upon looking, she found a dark-haired man standing in front of her, several inches taller and blocking the light just behind him, making it difficult for her to see who it was.

She took a step back, swallowing hard as she recognized the almond-shaped eyes and strong jaw, the lips she'd stared at a time or two all those years before. With his eyes on hers, her breath caught. With a nervous sweep of her hand, she brushed her hair back, feeling like a seventeen-year-old again.

"Sadie?"

Evan. His rich voice sent her straight back to her childhood when they would skip rocks along the pond by his house. Then her thoughts moved to high school where he was the popular guy every girl wanted to date. And finally, the day they graduated from Hawthorne when he'd led the graduates in a cheer as they waited to file into the stadium.

The memory of that night echoed in her brain, the hurt of it causing her heart to slow down a few beats. She remembered seeing him with another girl on his arm, even though he'd promised to take her to the after-party. It had been the culmination of so many little slights that she wished she could just move on.

"Yup. It's me." Holding up the ice bucket, she said, "Just going to get some ice."

They stood there in awkward silence for several moments, Sadie's heart pounding in her chest. Why would it betray her like that? She'd liked him when they were teenagers, but once they'd made it to Hawthorne, he'd become an arrogant jerk. That should be enough to tell her Evan Pearson wasn't the right guy for her. But then again, look at her family history. It wasn't like her parents had had a healthy relationship. Maybe she was destined for the same fate.

"You look great. It's been a while since I've seen you." He smiled, baring pearly white teeth that were exactly straight. She'd thought he'd gotten stronger throughout college with all the football training they were put through, but the man standing before her was even bigger, his shirt tight around his biceps.

What was she supposed to say to that? Thanks?

"You've been busy building this." She reached her hands out to the side and looked around as if to encompass the entire hotel with that gesture.

His hazel eyes stared at her, causing her to shift with discomfort. As if snapping out of some strange haze, he finally said, "Is everything okay with your room?"

She nodded. "Yes. It's quite the room. But after the weekend, I would prefer to move to a smaller room since Aubrey will be going to Aspen Hollow on Monday."

"No, you're planning my sister's wedding. It's the least I can do to make your stay comfortable. Besides, you'll probably have a lot of stuff to plan it, boards and supplies. Just stay in that one until the wedding."

With a shrug, Sadie said, "I'm not going to fight you on that." She smiled wide, and when he returned it, one side of his mouth considerably higher than the other, there was no holding back the feelings bearing down on the wall she'd built years ago to keep them back.

She took a step to the side, trying to move around him. If she stayed where she was, he'd be able to hear her traitorous heart, and she wasn't in the mood for his ego. Seven years and billions of dollars probably hadn't tamed it at all.

"Let me know if I can get you anything." Evan's voice echoed down the hall, and Sadie nodded as she looked back, wishing she could run away and not look like she was breaking out of some lockdown facility.

Turning the corner to the ice machine, she set the bucket on the ledge and pressed the button, wondering if she would be able to survive the next few weeks of planning with Evan around. She hadn't even been in the vicinity for five minutes before she was acting like a nervous schoolgirl.

Maybe it was because he was an attractive guy and she hadn't seen him in so long that her body had reacted like that. It wouldn't take long for his true colors to show, and then her attraction for him would die. At least, she hoped so.

CHAPTER 4

*E*van stood in the hall for a few moments before moving to the elevator and heading down. When was the last time he'd seen Sadie? He knew she and Aubrey roomed together at Hawthorne, and he remembered seeing her at graduation, but he hadn't visited the two of them since, usually only seeing his sister at home in Aspen Hollow for family occasions.

With her dark red hair and piercing green eyes, why hadn't he taken notice of her long ago? He'd always found auburn hair attractive, but she was Aubrey's best friend, and he'd known her since they were in grade school. But she definitely didn't look like that before. The girl he'd known had worn thick glasses and usually pulled her hair in a ponytail. This version of Sadie pulled at him, making him realize how blind he'd been all those years ago.

He'd come to their floor to check on another guest, not knowing Sadie and Aubrey had arrived. Not wanting to run into Sadie again or make things awkward, he'd gotten back into the elevator. It dinged as it reached the first floor, and

Evan pulled his phone out of his pocket, dialing his sister's number. She picked up on the first ring.

"Hey, Evan. Thanks for the awesome room."

"I heard you were enjoying it. When did you get in?"

"About thirty minutes ago. How'd you know we were here? Did George call you?" He could picture her face, eyes wide with surprise.

Walking toward his office, he said, "No, why? Did something happen to the car?"

"No, I just didn't see your manager, so I wasn't sure how you already knew."

Grinning, Evan took a seat at his desk and said, "This is my hotel. I have eyes everywhere. But this time, they were mine. I met Sadie walking to get ice."

"That's cheating." She laughed on the other end, causing Evan to do the same. "What's up?"

Remembering he had a reason for calling her, he said, "I was wondering if the two of you wanted to have dinner downstairs tonight. My treat."

"Yeah, I think we'd be up for that. Just a second. Sadie just came back with her filled bucket." Aubrey must have covered the end of the phone because he didn't hear anything for several seconds. What would they be talking about for so long? It was just a dinner for friends. Right?

"Okay, I'm back. How about that Italian place?"

"Sounds good." Evan grinned. "You two haven't changed."

"What? Pasta, bread. What's not to like?" Aubrey giggled. "Talk to Sadie. I've got to check something."

He could hear Sadie's laugh as the phone got closer to her. "Your sister is weird."

"This is true. But you're the one who has to put up with it all the time." He laughed, feeling more relaxed than he had in a while. "I'll meet you downstairs at seven." Evan leaned forward in his office chair.

"Better make the reservation, then," Sadie said. "Friday nights get busy."

"Not for the owner." He grinned wide, wondering what she thought of that.

She groaned. "Sounds like you haven't changed much yourself. We'll see you later."

He heard a click on the line and had to look to see that she'd hung up.

Had she meant that as a good thing? Something inside him decided it wasn't a compliment, and he wondered what she'd gotten offended about.

For some reason, he couldn't wait to meet them for dinner. As he thought back to bumping into Sadie in the hall, she'd done everything she could to get away from him. Such a contrast to all of the women he had to fend off at events or just as customers at his hotel. It was somewhat refreshing and had to be the reason why he felt off around her, both disconcerted and excited. He hadn't planned for this turn of events.

He was on track to winning the five-diamond award, and now was not the time to get distracted by a beautiful woman. It wasn't just his personal life that had taken a hit when Stacey had walked away, his businesses had also suffered. Now that he was back on track and excelling, so were each of his hotels. The five-diamond award was the crown jewel of what he hoped to build for his company and his employees. Achieving that meant ultimate focus on making sure every-thing went according to plan, not trying to divide his atten-tion with a new relationship.

As long as they didn't have to spend too much time together, things would return to normal, and he could go back to avoiding all women, even red-haired ones who popped up out of his past.

* * *

AFTER DRESSING FOR DINNER, buttoning a lavender shirt and pulling on a gray sport coat, Evan made his way downstairs, not wanting the girls to wait too long for him.

He arrived first but only had to wait a few minutes before he saw the two of them laughing as they walked toward him. A bit of envy pricked at his chest, and he felt the void of Aiden's absence. The two of them had been together for just about everything, even though they were different in so many ways. With his brother back in San Francisco, he felt the void. As much as he loved his sister, there was something about that identical bond that made it different.

He watched as Sadie tucked her hair behind one ear as she laughed at something Aubrey said, dressed in a pair of tailored black slacks and a navy top. With her hair down, he had to put a hand to his chest to keep his heart from galloping away. What had he been thinking? Dinner with her was going to make keeping his mind on his goals harder than he thought. And having to keep those feelings from his sister was going to be another feat in and of itself.

"You made it. Hey, Aubs," he said, hugging her.

"It's good to see you, Evan. I hope you've been staying out of trouble." She took a step back and studied his face using the look their mother usually gave them to root out any secret they'd been hiding.

"Trying to. I'm a workaholic, so there isn't too much to worry about around here." He stepped back and turned to Sadie. "It's good to see you again, Sadie."

She nodded. "Hello, Goose." She stuck out her hand rather quickly, and Evan took it, shaking it slowly as he studied her reaction. The look in her eyes went from surprise to bored in just a few seconds, causing him to finally pull away.

Aubrey started laughing. "I forgot about that one. It's been a long time since you two have been together."

Evan thought back to when they were about four years old and a goose had been waddling around the pond next to the ranch his parents owned. He'd gone up to it, trying to give it some bread like he'd seen other people do, but he put the bread right to the beak of the goose. His fingers had hurt for weeks after, and he'd been given the nickname of Goose by his family. Over the years, it had been replaced by other nicknames, but Sadie had never stopped using Goose.

"Leave it to Sadie to remember something that happened over two decades ago."

Sadie smiled. "Two decades. Are you trying to make us feel old?"

Evan tilted his head down, a smile playing at the corners of his lips. "You are a whole two weeks older than Aubrey and me."

"That makes no difference." She slapped his arm, and he noticed her shoulders relax a bit. "Okay, which direction? My stomach is going to riot soon if I don't get food."

Pointing in the direction of the stairs, Evan took a few steps forward, allowing the girls to fall into step with him.

He stuck one hand into his pants pocket and weaved around some people not paying attention in the hall. Looking over at Sadie, he said, "Taryn tells me you've got a little fan club going for your wedding planning business."

"A little fan club." She laughed, but it sounded hollow. "I caught a lucky break with Maleah Strong and an article in a magazine for a wedding I did in May, but I wouldn't say business is streaming in."

"But you've already had a few calls since Maleah's wedding. You're even going to plan one for Charleigh French," Aubrey said, beaming and turning her head to look at the ceiling lit to look just like the sky.

Evan was impressed. "Charleigh French, huh? I would say you've arrived, then."

With a shake of the head, Sadie rolled her eyes. "I don't have the contract with her yet. She wants to come to Taryn's wedding and see if she likes it. She and her fiancé were at Maleah's wedding. I just wish I didn't have that extra pressure on top of a short time frame." She bit her bottom lip, her eyes straight forward as if trying to look into the future.

"I'm sure you'll do just fine," Evan said. "Taryn says she trusts you completely."

Sadie looked at him for several seconds, her eyes moving around his face as if inspecting every part of it for a lie. When she finally spoke, her voice was near a whisper. "Thank you for that."

Evan wasn't sure what she meant by that, but something about her manner told him not to press it. At least he'd gotten a thank you.

CHAPTER 5

Sadie tried to keep her thoughts on the food, savoring the rich sauces and soft bread of the restaurant. While she did enjoy the food, she kept glancing up to study Evan, trying to reconcile the guy she remembered from all those years ago with the guy who sat before her. There seemed to be a peace about him, but she wasn't sure what had caused it.

She'd known about his broken engagement, and when Aubrey commented several months later that he still hadn't gotten over it, that had stuck in Sadie's brain. She saw no sign of it now, but it was as if he was seeing her for the first time.

His jaw was more defined, and a scar along his forearm piqued her curiosity. He must have gotten it after college since she'd never seen it before. Other than that, the brown eyes with large flecks of green and long eyelashes made her insides buzz. But it was the smile that really got her. He'd never needed braces, and yet his teeth were perfect, unlike her own.

Glancing back at her plate of pasta, she twirled her fork

through a few pieces of alfredo. Frustration webbed through her chest. Evan was a slippery slope she couldn't fall down again. She had to be grateful he'd been such a jerk those last few years in college, since it had broken the trance she'd been in over him. Whatever it was he'd been going through at that time, she knew it was for the best that he was rude and a player, for more than one reason.

She'd thought things must have changed drastically for him to marry Stacey Crenshaw, a girl from their high school who'd dated him on and off throughout the years, but when the wedding was called off hours before it was set to happen, she'd felt a sense of both triumph and sadness about the whole situation. Stacey had always been a piece of work, the head cheerleader and leader of the mean girls' clique, but as much as Sadie liked the thought that it didn't work out for her, she felt even worse for Evan. Maybe that was what caused her heart to lean toward him, that life hadn't turned out exactly how he'd planned it, and she could relate to that.

Aubrey had filled her in on a lot of what had happened in the succeeding weeks, including Evan's struggle to get back to work. He must have gotten over Stacey, or at least funneled his frustrations into his business, because Sadie couldn't imagine what it would have taken to get to the billion-dollar mark soon after. It wasn't something she cared about, and when he'd made the remark about things being easy as the owner, she knew he hadn't changed all that much. His arrogant, cocky attitude was still in full force.

"Evan, are you coming home for the fall festival?" Aubrey asked before taking a bite of her pasta.

"I'll be there. Mom would hang me if I didn't make it this time. She said they're expecting to be sold out of rooms at the lodge for the weekend." Evan's eyes danced at that. He had grown up on a large ranch in Southern Utah, the land having been passed down from generation to generation from the time his great-grandfather had settled there. Over the years, the Pearson family had built a lodge where they hosted family reunions or corporate retreats, allowing their guests to experience the ranch life for a few days or weeks.

Sadie wished she could feel the same excitement for the big event as the Pearsons did. All the Fall Festival meant for her was disappointment and heartache.

Aubrey pointed her fork in Sadie's direction. "Maybe you can convince this one to come along for once. It's been a long time." She raised her eyebrows as if to emphasize the point.

Evan lifted his hands. "If you can't convince her to go, what makes you think I can?" He chuckled, and the sound was warm and comfortable.

"I can hear you," Sadie said, glaring at him across the table. After a moment, she sat back against the seat of the booth. "There's nothing left for me in Aspen Hollow. It's just easier to not go back and see all the pitying stares." Sadie could feel the emotion surging in her throat, causing her to look down so she wouldn't start crying. She hadn't been this emotional in ages, and she wished it would go away. She'd been able to steel herself against the memories of the past for a while and didn't need Aubrey constantly bringing them back up.

"What if you could finally get over your anxiety about Aspen Hollow? You'll be with us the entire time, and then you can have some of Mom's Dutch apple pie. I know you have to be missing that." One side of Aubrey's mouth lifted.

Sadie nodded. "Okay, I might be missing that. But I don't know if I'm quite ready to go back just yet. Maybe next year." She noted the finality in her tone, and the rightness of it surged through her. "Besides, I have a wedding to throw together in about five weeks. If I'm going to impress Charleigh, I've got to stay focused."

She was surprised to see Evan staring at her with his lips

pressed into a tight line. A light tingle flowed down her back, and she averted her eyes. Twirling the last of her pasta around her fork, Sadie wondered what he was thinking. She hoped it was something about this large hotel and not about her past. He hadn't learned about most of it, of her parents fighting the last few years of their marriage and then filing restraining orders against one another.

Her parents had never been the model of an amazing marriage, but those last several months, Sadie had avoided the courtroom like the plague, knowing that each appearance would only cause her to lose respect for her parents even more. There was one particular time that she could never forget, like it was seared into her brain.

Shaking her head, she tried to figure out what Evan and Aubrey were saying. She needed a distraction from those old memories more than ever.

CHAPTER 6

With working to line up several subcontractors for the remodel over the weekend, Evan had only seen Sadie once, on his way out of the gym downstairs. She'd been across the room, pacing as she talked on her phone about something to do with Taryn's big day. The minute he'd heard the word wedding, he'd turned and focused on the elevator, hoping it would keep him out of an awkward conversation about his former life. He had an urge to tell her about everything that had happened to him over the past seven or even eleven years, but that was something a boyfriend did, not an old acquaintance.

Sunday afternoon, Sadie walked into his office, a large three-ring binder in her hands. "Good afternoon. Can you give me the number for your events coordinator? I want to set some things up for the few days before the wedding. To give the guests that come early a fun experience."

With a grin, Evan said, "That sounds like a great idea. Let me have her call you later today. She's been sick recently, but I hope she'll be able to help out in planning."

"Awesome. Okay, I'll leave you to your work and get back

to planning this wedding." She turned and then paused, looking back at him. "You weren't kidding when you said you're a workaholic."

Throwing back his head, Evan laughed. After several seconds, he stopped, again realizing he didn't know if that was a compliment or a jab. "Getting a hotel started is a big job, and it means hiring the right people and training them on how our hotels are supposed to treat customers."

"Where are you on this hotel, then?" Evan could see the curiosity playing in her eyes.

"I bought it two years ago and have been remodeling since. One of my friends from college has a girlfriend who is a designer, and she flew out a month ago to help me pick out new furnishings and a few other details for the hotel. This has been a lot more of a process than the other hotels I own around the country. And with all of the extra shops and features of the place, I would say I'm about halfway done training people." He paused a moment before saying, "What about you? You're busy working on a Sunday. Doesn't that make you a workaholic too?"

A smile played on her lips, and Evan found it adorable. "No, I just have a very tight deadline. But it is sometimes easier to get lost in the little details rather than figure out people. Aubrey and I already went to lunch, and she's taking care of a few things before she heads to Aspen Hollow tomorrow."

"Point taken. What is it about Aspen Hollow that keeps you from returning? I know your parents had a rough patch, but what makes you stay away?" He watched as several emotions flickered across her face.

It took her several seconds to respond, but she finally said, "There's just a lot of memories I wish to forget. The whole house-burning thing is one of them."

Evan searched his mind, trying to remember what she

was talking about. It seemed like one of those memories that hadn't been dusted off in a while. "I almost forgot about that. I just remember you staying over for several nights because you couldn't sleep there anymore. That was when we were, what? Sixteen."

Sadie nodded. "My parents were fighting so much about who got the house that one of them decided to burn it down."

"Are you serious? When was that?"

Sadie sighed, looking to the shelves behind him as she thought. "The year before we graduated from high school. The minute college started, I was ready to leave that town, and I haven't been back since."

"Were you able to salvage anything from the fire?" He thought about his own possessions. What would he be able to save if a fire happened here in the hotel?

Her lips turned down, and she shook her head. "No, it was too late when the firefighters made it to the house. I'm just grateful none of us were hurt. It made for a long couple of years, though."

"Where are your parents now?" Evan didn't want her to stop talking, as a lot of little pieces started to fall into place. His mother had probably explained the situation to him on several occasions, but he hadn't had time to worry about things at home in a few years. Now he wished he'd paid better attention to what he'd always termed as mindless gossip.

"My father is in North Carolina, and my mother lives in Boise. Shannon stayed in Colorado after grad school."

"Do you ever see any of them?"

Sadie shook her head. "Not often. My parents both got remarried and have their own lives now. I've been busy with all the weddings lately. If I'm in the area, I try to stop by or arrange a lunch, but that doesn't happen often."

Evan ran a hand along the back of his neck. "That seems so foreign to me. My mother calls every time she hasn't heard from me in a while. Do you miss them?"

With a shrug, Sadie said, "Sometimes, but there was just so much stuff going on at the time that it's nice to be on the other side. And Shannon, well, I feel like Aubrey is more of a sister at this point."

The sadness on her face made his chest hurt. As much as his family seemed overwhelming at times, life wouldn't be the same without them. It made him want to visit them more often, to make sure he never took them for granted.

She waved a hand at him. "I have to get back to this. I have several phone calls to make and plans to go over with your sister."

Evan nodded, watching her walk out the door. It was a wonder that a girl with such a rough past when it came to her parents' marriage was now a sought-after wedding planner.

Reminding himself to call Patty, his events coordinator, he picked up the phone and dialed her number. After a few rings, she picked up, her voice hoarse and shaky.

"Hi, Patty, I was going to ask how you were feeling, but it doesn't sound like it's going all that well."

"I'm in the hospital with pneumonia, and I'm not sure how long I will be in here. I won't be back to work for a few weeks."

Evan's mind started spinning, thinking of all the things that were already planned for that time. "No worries. I'll take care of it so you can get better. Is everything on your calendar up-to-date?"

"Yes. It has the names of the parties and should have numbers listed so you can contact them to confirm. I'm sorry, Mr. Pearson."

"Don't be sorry. Just take whatever time you need to get

well. And let me know if you need anything from me. I'll make sure to send it over as soon as you request it." He smiled as she thanked him and hung up.

How was he going to get everything done that he needed to? It wouldn't be worth it to hire someone to take over Patty's place for now. Evan had trained her on the system, and it would take just as long to train someone as it would be for him to do it. With all of the subcontractors lined up, he would just need to check in every once in a while as he fielded calls for events.

Evan stepped into the hall and spoke with his secretary, Janice. "Patty is out for the next few weeks. Will you have all the calls for events run through my phone? I'll be taking charge of it during that time."

The lady with gray streaks in her hair raised an eyebrow. "Are you sure you'll be able to sleep if you take that on? With the schedule you already have, it's a wonder you're getting any beauty rest as it is."

Laughing, Evan nodded. "This is true. But I have a bunch of things already set up for the remodel, and I'm hoping it will just be maintenance. I'll just have to be fluid."

"I'm booking you a vacation the minute she comes back. It's not healthy for a young man to only be working."

Some time off sounded perfect right then. But he'd have to push forward, hoping he'd make it through at least the wedding and holidays before that could happen.

With one more call to make, he dialed Sadie's number as he walked to Patty's office. When she answered, he said, "It looks like we'll be working together. I'm the events coordinator for now."

CHAPTER 7

Sadie still couldn't believe she'd told Evan all of that. But then again, knowing his mother, he probably knew most of it already. She could imagine he hadn't deemed it important information in the first place and had just gone about his merry way.

And now she had to work with him. She'd been feeling good about keeping him at arm's length, knowing he'd be in the hotel but she wouldn't have to see him on a daily basis. Now, that seemed like a pipe dream.

She made it back to the small conference room on the first floor where she'd set up a temporary office. As nice as the suite was where she was staying, it seemed like she got more done in the simpler space and could see more with the samples spread over the table.

Taryn would be done with her conference in the next hour or two and would come by and approve several of the decorations Sadie had picked out for her, allowing enough time for the orders to come in. She had hoped to have some preliminary activities set up, but she wasn't sure Evan could come up with sensible ideas.

The door opened, and Sadie looked up to see Taryn walking into the room. She looked as amazing as ever, dressed in workout clothes and looking as though she'd just applied her makeup. If Sadie looked like that after even thirty minutes of working out, let alone the whole day, she might work out more often.

Taryn held out her arms and pulled Sadie in for a hug. After several seconds, she pulled back and said, "Sadie! It's been forever. It's so good to see you, and thank you again for doing my wedding on such short notice. It's such a relief to have someone I can depend on."

"I'm excited to share what I've come up with so far," Sadie said, waving her hand over the table of samples and ideas as Taryn took a seat next to the conference table. "Since we have about five weeks until the big day, we need to get some of the bigger decisions hammered out today so I can get things ordered."

"Great idea. I have a couple of hours until my flight, so I'm all ears." She reached forward and touched a sample of lace. "I like this. What were you thinking of using it for?"

This was Sadie's favorite part, mapping out the vision for the wedding and then tweaking it based on what the bride wanted.

"I know you said you wanted to keep things more low-key now that your wedding will be here, so I started thinking of—"

The door opened again, and Evan walked in, dressed in a maroon polo shirt and dark gray slacks. Sadie ducked her head so he wouldn't see her cheeks redden at the sight of his toned arms and the short scruff on his face.

"What's up, Evan? How'd you know we were in here?" Taryn asked, swiveling her chair to the side. She leaned her chin on her hand, narrowing her eyes at her younger brother. Sadie wished she could muster that much intimidation.

"A guy can't come and see his sister?" Evan asked, raising his hands in the air. When she didn't respond, he said, "Brent told me you'd arrived. I'm acting as events coordinator for the hotel for a few weeks and figured it might be a good time to go over things so we can get them scheduled out."

Sadie looked for mocking in his expression but found he was actually serious. He placed a folder on the table in front of him and opened it, flipping through several pages until he got to the page he needed.

Irritation bubbled up inside her. Trying to keep her tone even, Sadie said, "I appreciate you trying to put all of this together right now, but there are a lot of details I need to discuss with Taryn before she leaves. Can you arrange this over the phone?"

Evan's gaze turned to Sadie, an arrogant smile playing on his lips. What she ever saw in him, she didn't know.

"I guess we can. I'm just trying to get things figured out so I don't screw it up."

The self-deprecation in his voice hit Sadie in the chest, thawing some of the frustration she'd felt at him trying to take over their meeting. A bit of insecurity flashed across his face before a polite smile took over.

Looking at her phone for the time, Sadie said, "Okay, I will make sure to leave at least thirty minutes to discuss activities for the wedding. Do you want us to call you when we're done discussing lace and ribbon?" She raised an eyebrow and waited for his response.

"It might be good for me to listen in so I can gain some experience in wedding planning, just in case Patty is ever sick again." His smile was close-lipped, and Sadie wondered if he had an ulterior motive or if he was sincere.

"I'd say you had plenty of experience from your own wedding, but I think Stacey did most of that for you."

Taryn's words sounded harsh to Sadie's ears, and as she watched Evan, sympathy formed inside her. His jaw worked back and forth, and his Adam's apple bobbed a few times. His eyes narrowed as he pulled out a chair next to Taryn, sitting down without breaking his gaze away from his sister.

Taryn didn't seem to notice the play of emotions as she'd already turned back to the table. "Actually, it might be good to have you here, just to get a male perspective. You and Travis have similar tastes, so it will help me focus a little more."

Over the next hour and a half, they worked to refine the design of the wedding and get the materials figured out, and Sadie had a good list of Taryn's thoughts as they talked about the items. They would ask Evan his thoughts every so often, and he would give them, looking like he'd resigned himself to an hour of misery. Was he just reliving his own failed wedding?

"I want some kind of dancing space for the reception. I'd like to have all the traditional father-daughter and mother-son dances but then invite others to join us at the end."

Biting her bottom lip, Sadie nodded, trying to figure out how to make that work. She'd have to sneak back into the event room and measure a few things. After writing it down on her to-do list, she looked up and said, "I'll call around to see if someone has one that would work for this space." She gave Taryn a reassuring smile, the one that kept the feelings of not-sure-she-could-deliver deep down and giving the bride the confidence that it would get done. "Okay, as far as the wedding gown goes, have you already been shopping for one?"

Taryn nodded. "Does it count if it was for fun five years ago?"

Sadie groaned and rolled her eyes. "No. We should plan to shop for one in the next week or so. Would you like me to arrange for your mother to come here and go with you?"

"I'd like that. I'm flying back to California for a couple of days, but I'm thinking about going back to Aspen Hollow for the festival this next weekend. Maybe we could go look at some places there or in St. George after it's all over."

Shrugging, Sadie said, "I could meet you in St. George. I really want to get things taken care of, and if I take time off to head back to Aspen Hollow, it will derail the momentum we have going right now."

"I think it would be best for Sadie to refresh her memory on some of the rustic stuff," Evan said with a mischievous grin.

"What's that supposed to mean?" Sadie shot back, heat rising up her neck.

"Just that it might do you some good to see Silver Ridge Ranch again. Mom told me she's been baking for days, and she's already finished a bunch of the crafts she makes. You can't tell me you haven't missed our mom's cooking." His eyebrows raised, and the one corner of his mouth lifted ever so slightly, making her insides feel like they were taking off for a hundred-meter dash.

"Really? You're over there in designer clothes with your fingers manicured, and you're saying I need to see the ranch? I was there so often growing up that it was burned into my memory."

Taryn and Evan started laughing at the same time, leaving Sadie to look between them, wondering what she'd said that was so funny.

"What?" she finally asked, annoyed more than usual.

"Girl, I get why you are best friends with Aubrey," Taryn said, trying to catch her breath. "I mean, I always knew you were two peas in a pod, but the way you put Evan in his place right then was spectacular. I give it a high nine."

Evan's laugh eased into a wide smile. "Manicured hands. That would require me to touch lotion. Gross."

It was Sadie's turn to join in on the laughter as his look of disgust and tone of his voice surprised her.

"Maybe we should all go see the ranch. I'm sure Mom and Dad would love having a mini-reunion. Aubrey will be heading that way soon." Taryn pulled out her phone and tapped the calendar app, scrolling through a long list of things to do. "I'll rearrange some of this so we can attend. Evan, get Aiden to come into town. It will be a nice surprise to have us all home before the wedding."

A pit formed in Sadie's stomach, and she knew what it was from. Why were the Pearsons so insistent on making her go back to the place that fueled her nightmares? She wanted to scream, wanted to run upstairs and lock the door and come out only after the festival was over.

"Sounds like a good plan. We can drive over on Thursday afternoon." Evan was looking at her, and as much as a part of her was curious what a two-and-a-half-hour drive with Evan would be like, she couldn't do it.

Shaking her head, she said, "Not this time. I've got to make sure everything is all taken care of, and the days are ticking by faster and faster. But you can always bring me back a piece of your mom's pie." She wiggled her eyebrows and gave them a thumbs up, hoping to steer things in another direction with her joke.

"No can do," Evan said. "Mom's apple pie must be eaten warm, and that's a long drive to get it back to you."

"It's called a microwave, Goose." She paused a few seconds before she turned back to the samples, noting the last few Taryn had selected.

"Is it my turn to talk about events?" Evan asked, his loud sigh causing Sadie to smile.

She waved her hand in his direction. "Plan away. I'm interested to see what you come up with."

CHAPTER 8

*A*fter saying goodbye to Aubrey on Monday morning, it seemed as if Evan's phone was ringing all week. Most of the calls were for the events coordinator, either from current guests asking what they could participate in during their stay or future customers inquiring about scheduling activities. When Patty returned, she deserved a raise for all she had to put up with.

The painters he'd hired had shown up on Tuesday morning, allowing him to breathe a bit easier as progress was happening. He didn't want to let his sister down and knew that if the large room wasn't finished, his mother wouldn't let him forget it.

He'd seen Sadie a few times, usually in the conference room as she laid out different materials or typed while on the phone. As much as he felt drawn to her, he kept fighting the urge, hoping the small attraction would stay just that. There was no way he could get involved with another woman. If Stacey hadn't wanted him, who was to say anyone else would be interested, let alone in for the long haul?

They'd been together on and off throughout high school

and had reconnected soon after he'd graduated Hawthorne. It was as if everything clicked into place, and they'd gotten engaged quickly. Preparations for their wedding took about six months, and he'd been so ready to start his life with her. But it had been too good to last, and in some ways, he was grateful it hadn't worked out. It had been a long process, getting over her, but after hearing that she was already divorced, he felt vindicated. It was for the best.

From what Evan had learned about Sadie's parents, it sounded like marriage was tainted for her as well. He was grateful his parents had a strong marriage, giving and taking when they needed in order to make it work. If only he could find someone and know for a surety that she wouldn't break his heart.

Maybe Sadie was that person, but from her sentiments about weddings, she did it for the love of planning and designing rather than because she was ready to settle down. He had no idea what it would be like to suffer through his parents' divorce, and the fact that her family didn't see each other much now baffled him. As much as he worked at the hotel and the other businesses he owned, it still seemed like his family got together enough to keep that bond strong.

Sadie had asked for a list of the activities he'd decided on with Taryn the other day. She'd left to check on some boxes that had come in at the front desk and missed the discussion. He walked into the conference room on Tuesday afternoon and laid it down in front of her. She was on the phone and held up her finger, so he sat down. He glanced over the layers of lace and color swatches lying on the table while he waited.

When she got off the phone, she lifted the paper and looked at it for several seconds before turning to him. "Are these the activities Taryn wanted?" The three of them had spent so much time on Sunday with the details and then the debate about heading to Aspen Hollow that he'd only had about fifteen minutes to go over a list of options they had at the hotel before Taryn had to leave to catch her flight.

Nodding, Evan said, "Yeah. I was surprised with some of them myself, but if that's what she wants to do, I'll just schedule it."

Sadie rolled her lips in and shook her head. "No, there's no way your family is going to want to go to all of those shows beforehand. What day is everyone coming into town?"

"They're coming in four days before the ceremony, so Sunday? Taryn said that's what she wants everyone to partic-ipate in."

Shaking her head, Sadie said, "Sometimes brides have tunnel vision. They're so excited about the big day that they don't really think about the people around them. Not that doing that will make them into bridezilla, but a little persua-sion by a third party can make it even better."

Folding his arms across his chest, Evan tilted his head and looked at her for a few seconds. "So what do you suggest?"

"Do you have a complete list of events your hotel provides?"

Evan slid another sheet over to her, and she lifted it up, glancing through the different activities and the business they were connected to.

"Okay, your parents and grandparents are not going to want to go skydiving, nor will they want to watch the teeny-bopper singer you've got during those dates. Think about them. What would they enjoy?" She slid the paper back over to him, and he could feel her eyes on him as he concentrated. She had a point, but he definitely wasn't skilled in events enough to have a better plan. He'd have to spend more of his precious time going through it.

* * *

SADIE COULDN'T PULL her eyes away from Evan, feeling a small collection of butterflies fluttering in her stomach. Breaking her stare, she pulled out a few other papers and waited for his response.

There was no reason to be attracted to him again. He had a bazillion dollars and was just as arrogant as ever. With Sadie's stubbornness, they would never survive as a couple. Not that it would even be an option. She'd always been Aubrey's best friend, and at that moment, she had to remember the reason she'd promised herself not to marry years ago. Even then, she'd known it would all end in disaster.

But there was that sincerity she'd seen several times already, something he hadn't shown in college. Even now, as he looked over the paper, she wondered if his broken relationship had really changed him that much.

"My grandparents would love some kind of luau or something to get the whole family together. My parents would enjoy that as well, although excursions for the guys and girls might be a good option." He looked up at her, studying her face.

Sadie smiled and pointed to him. "Bingo! So for the dinner rehearsal, we'll do something like a luau or just a big dinner. Will the event room be open during that time?"

It took a moment for Evan to answer, and when he did, it was as if his mind had been somewhere else. "The night before? Yeah, it should be, barring no delays in finishing the remodel."

"Okay, is there somewhere you can take the guys? You could rent some UTVs or even go shooting somewhere on the outskirts of Las Vegas. The girls would love a spa day, manicures, pedicures, etc."

Evan smiled, his bright white teeth shining against his

lightly tanned skin. "That actually sounds like a great idea. I'm impressed."

Raising an eyebrow, Sadie said, "You didn't think I could do this? It's my job to read people and what they want most."

His smile turned mischievous, and he leaned on the table, only a foot away from her now. "Really? So what do you see in me?"

Waving her hand in the air, Sadie shook her head. Pulling the papers back into order, she tapped them onto the table-top, making them all straight. "No, I don't share my obser-vations."

"Why not? I'm really curious as to what you think of me and what I could possibly want."

Looking into his eyes, Sadie debated whether or not to divulge her inner thoughts. "It's been a long time since we've seen each other, and I'm still building a profile for you."

"You can't give me one little tidbit of information? Just your first impression." He paused but continued when he saw she wasn't going to budge. "What were your thoughts after I said the bit about getting a restaurant with ease because I'm the owner?"

Sadie laughed, not really wanting to go into it, but she knew he wasn't going to let it go.

"Honestly, I thought you were the same arrogant jerk you were in college. Of course, you throw your weight and money around so people flock to you and you get whatever you want."

His jaw went slack for several seconds before his mask appeared and he sat back. She saw the muscles tense around his jaw, knowing she'd hit a nerve.

"Thank you for your assessment. I'll need to prove that I've changed at least a bit in the past seven years." His smile looked forced, and he stood up, pushing his chair back in.

Sadie reached out, aiming for his forearm but grabbing

his hand instead. "Evan," she began, trying to push the little sparks flowing through her fingers out of her mind. "I'm sure you've changed since then. You were pushing me to tell you something."

One corner of his mouth turned up, and his eyes locked onto hers for what felt like minutes, the green showing through more than normal. "You're good, Sadie. I guess it's just been a while since someone has called me out on that. As hard as it is to accept that I'm not perfect, it will be better in the long run."

He looked down at their hands, and Sadie wondered if he felt the same tingles now running up her arm. She dropped her hand to her lap, throwing back the length of her ponytail with the other.

With a sigh, she said, "Just know, I have plenty of faults myself. I just hope you don't think I don't see that as well."

Evan's smile deepened, looking a bit sad. "I think we've both been through quite a lot. Maybe it's time to rebuild and move forward." He turned and waved as he left the room.

Sadie's cheeks were on fire, and she dropped her head into her hands. Leave it to her to drive people away, even those who were like family and were just trying to help. She'd have to find a way to apologize to him later. Even if there was no future for them, she wanted a better relationship with Evan.

CHAPTER 9

Thursday afternoon, Evan knocked on Sadie's door. She'd texted him earlier with a message that she needed to talk, but he'd searched the hotel in all her usual haunts, and this was the last place he could think of to look. Now that he stood before the door, he should have texted back to see where she was. But looking for her had allowed him to put off calling back one of his future clients about booking fifty people for one of the hotel's excursions. He wasn't in the mood to type so many names into the system.

The door swung open, and Sadie walked away, saying, "Hi," over her shoulder before she moved into the bedroom. Evan hesitated a few seconds before he stepped inside and closed the door. He opened his mouth to say something, when she walked back out, wheeling a small suitcase.

"Are you going somewhere?" he asked, looking back at her face. Her lips were pulled taut in a thin line.

She let go of the handle and crossed her arms over her chest. "Apparently, I'm going to Aspen Hollow with you."

He frowned, trying to decide if this was all some big joke.

"I don't understand. I thought you said you weren't going and would never go back to Aspen Hollow."

"It turns out Taryn can be very persuasive. She only has time to shop for a wedding dress while she's there." She let out a sigh, and Evan did everything he could to keep a smile from crossing his face.

"Can't she just go with our mom?"

Sadie pointed to him like he'd won the jackpot. "That's exactly what I said. But she wants me to be able to help your mom envision what we've got planned. When are you leaving?"

"In about an hour." He reached forward and took her bag. "I can take this downstairs now if you want. I just have a few more things to tie up before we head out."

"Just a minute. Let me make sure I packed everything I need in there."

She disappeared into the bedroom, and Evan took a seat on the couch, glad he'd splurged for the more comfortable couches in these suites rather than the board-like ones that weren't comfortable for anyone. But then again, that was Isabelle Rousseau's idea, and her input had been worth every penny it had taken to fly her here from London for the consultation.

Rolling out another suitcase, Sadie said, "Okay, I think we'll need that box over there," she pointed to the box next to him on the floor, "and the one over here by the door."

"You need all that? I thought we were just going for the weekend." What could she need with all this stuff? As his mind puzzled over that, his eyes caught on her figure wearing a pair of jeans that fit just right around her curves and a green t-shirt. She'd changed quite a bit over the years, and Evan felt a tug toward her, like she was someone he needed to get to know on a deeper level than just his sister's friend.

"Yeah, I'm planning to have your mom and Aubrey help me put together a gift I'm planning. It will be a surprise for Taryn, so we'll have to think of some kind of diversion to get her out of the house for a while."

Grinning, Evan said, "I think I can handle it. A trail ride would be great for that."

Sadie laughed. "It's hard to believe you still enjoy horseback riding."

"It helps clear my head better than running on the treadmill, but I've had to use the treadmill for the last few years." He rolled his eyes, and she laughed, the sound sweet and light, making him want to do something else so it would continue. "I can't wait to have some time to relax this weekend."

"Good luck with that," she said, a smirk on her face. "You do remember how into the Fall Festival your mother gets, right? I bet you'll be moving things all weekend."

Evan thought about the festival from the year before, but he'd only been able to make it for a day because of everything he'd been putting together for one of his other hotels. He nodded, remembering how she was for every holiday and knowing it would probably be just the same.

"Is everything set with the painters? They'll finish next week, right?" Sadie glanced up at him while she packed a jacket into the suitcase next to him.

Shaking his head, Evan said, "No, probably the next. I'll make sure they work on the event room first, though. It's just a big space, and I don't want to rush them. It's no use having to pay for it to get fixed again later."

Picking up the boxes, he waited as she opened the door, and then he walked out, barely able to see over his cargo. Sadie pressed the button to the elevator, and it opened fairly quickly, for which he was grateful. The boxes weren't super heavy, but even his reserved parking space was a bit of a walk.

"A Tahoe, huh?" Sadie said as he dropped the boxes at the rear of his SUV. "I'm surprised you didn't get a forest-green color. That was always your favorite."

Evan was surprised she remembered that. Had he ever known what her favorite color was? As he realized the answer was no, it sank in just how much he'd been into himself all those years ago.

"I like it. It has enough room for everything I need, whether it's for my business or for fun. Parking can get tricky here in the city, but then I just use George. The man is a master at parallel parking, even in the limo."

He unlocked the car and loaded the boxes and her suitcase as Sadie slid into the passenger seat. After shutting the rear door, Evan walked up and jumped into the driver's seat. Pulling out of the parking space, he put on his sunglasses in preparation for leaving the darkness.

"I think this is the most casual I've seen you in a long time: jeans and a t-shirt. Even your old Hawthorne football hat. I like it," Sadie said, smiling.

He watched her face, noting the slight change of her features as she beamed. She had a simple beauty that drew him even more than he'd thought possible. Not that he knew all that much about makeup, but it seemed she didn't wear much. Her lips looked naturally rosy, and he caught himself staring as he thought about what it would be like to kiss them. He was grateful he'd already put on the sunglasses so she couldn't see him blush.

"I like being comfortable when I drive." He glanced over his shoulder and located the bag of goodies on the floor of the back seat. "Will you grab one of those drinks out of the bag back there?"

She reached back and pulled out a red sports drink. Their fingers brushed as she handed it to him, and the ripple from her touch was like the sparks of a firework sparkler as it traveled up his skin. Had it just been a while since he'd dated anyone, and now he was falling for the first girl who stirred feelings inside him?

"Thank you," he said.

He took a sip as he waited for traffic to clear so they could head down the road to the freeway. Glancing at the clock, he knew they'd have to add an extra thirty to forty-five minutes onto their trip since they were leaving during rush hour.

"Do you want to get something for dinner? Or just get on the road?" he asked, peeking over at her and then turning his focus back to the road.

"Looks like we have a bunch of snacks already in here, so I should be fine." She pulled the rest of the bag into view and asked, "Did you get all of this?"

Giving her a joking grin, he said, "I requested it be brought over. My assistant is really good at getting things like that put together."

"She must already know about me, then, because she included beef jerky and sunflower seeds." Sadie grinned.

Evan chuckled, surprised that the information wasn't foreign to him. "I think anyone who's ever come into contact with you would know how much you love beef jerky."

"True, but most people don't remember that I like—"

"Peppered," Evan broke in to finish for her.

Looking surprised, Sadie nodded. "Maybe you aren't as bad as I always thought."

Evan grinned and tried to keep his eyes on the road, even though he could feel her eyes on him as they drove down the road, and for once, he would have given the bulk of his wealth to know what she was thinking.

"Well, I don't know your favorite color like you do mine, but there are a few things I'll always remember about you." He glanced over at her, trying to read her expression.

She turned in his direction as much as the seat belt would allow and said, "Really? I'm curious."

"When we were juniors in high school, you had a sleepover with Aubrey at our house. Aiden and I snuck in and put grasshoppers in your beds. Aubrey was screaming her head off and woke up the house. You just went and found a jar to collect them and release them out the window." He smiled wide and turned to her. "I was impressed that you didn't freak out, or crush the little guys."

Her eyes went unfocused, and it was a few seconds before she spoke. "My dad used to take us girls camping a lot to give my mom a break since he worked so much during the week. He'd make the insects seem fascinating, like they were just like us only on a smaller scale. I've never really been scared of them." The wistfulness in her voice disappeared with the faraway look, and she narrowed her eyes. "I knew that was the two of you. It was your mission to make us squeal when we had sleepovers."

"I think I only remember one time when Aubrey slept over at your house. In fact, you spent a lot of dinners with us in those later years. Is that when things got bad with your parents?" He took in a breath, hoping he wasn't overstepping his bounds. As close as they'd been while growing up, there were a lot of things—more serious, personal things—they'd never shared. It made him curious if Sadie had shared them with Aubrey at the time.

She nodded, her expression somber. "There were days when I just didn't want to go home because all it turned into was fighting. Sometimes I wondered why they stayed together so long after that. My mom waited for me to graduate from high school before she moved out of Aspen Hollow."

"She didn't wait for your sister to graduate?" Evan turned the wheel, getting onto the highway that would take them from Nevada to Utah.

"No," Sadie said, shaking her head. "She was four years younger and hadn't started high school yet. She did a lot better in Colorado, making some friends that were a good fit for her."

"When's the last time you've been back? To Aspen Hollow, I mean."

"Honestly, Christmas of freshman year of college. My mom was living over in Cherry Creek, and we came over for the Christmas program. I got an internship in St. George for the following summer and then just made sure I was occupied for all the other vacations and breaks. Things were just never the same after the fire."

Evan mulled that over. He remembered it being a big deal in their small town. From what he could remember, her parents had been fighting over who would get the home. Her father had come back from the bar and spread gasoline around the perimeter, sending the home into flames within minutes. By the time the volunteer firefighters made it out there, seventy-five percent of the house had been burned.

From the pain on Sadie's face, Evan knew she was reliving it. On impulse, he reached over and held her hand, squeezing it to help reassure her. The same sparks from a few minutes before flooded through him, and for once, he felt settled, like there was a possibility for a happy ending in his life. Whether that meant he needed Sadie in it or not, he wasn't sure, but right now, he was just a friend trying to comfort her.

She gave him a small smile and stared out the windshield

as the city traffic finally broke and he turned on cruise control as they sailed down the interstate.

"I know I haven't always been the best listener, but I'm open whenever you need me. Especially this weekend. We should have some sort of code that signals you need a break."

She laughed again, her face lighting up. He loved it when she smiled, and he felt a part of himself wanting to open up to her more.

"What should we say for the symbol? Goose?" he asked.

"That wouldn't work because that's what I call you."

He smiled. "And for some reason, it doesn't bug me when you say it." The air seemed to thicken, and he knew he had to pull back, make things a little lighter. He wasn't ready to be dating, and it sounded like she was still hurting from wounds long in her past. But they could be friends and help each other through the next few weeks.

"How about corn dogs?"

"What? Why would I say that?" Evan scrunched his nose in disgust.

"Exactly. It will be a sign you'll recognize because I know how much you dislike them." She raised her eyebrows, a smile on her face as she waited for his response.

Nodding as he tried to decide, he finally said, "Sounds good. Anytime you say corn dogs, I'll know you need to get out of whatever situation we're in. Got it?"

"Got it."

"Now I'm curious as to what we'll have to say so people won't be surprised by it."

Sadie chuckled, her shoulders shaking in the process. "I can only imagine what that will be like."

Evan grinned. "Knowing my family, any number of things."

They continued to drive, talking idly about this and that. Evan was grateful to have someone along for the ride. He felt comfortable with Sadie, and it didn't seem odd that he was starting to like the girl next to him. She had spunk and wouldn't let him get away with anything just because he was Evan Pearson, the billionaire. It was refreshing, like a cool wind on a hot Vegas day.

CHAPTER 10

Knots formed in Sadie's stomach and kept tightening as they drove closer to their small hometown. As they took the long two-lane road from the freeway back to Aspen Hollow, her throat seemed to narrow, and getting air in and out seemed like an impossible task.

At one point, Evan reached over again, holding her hand as she took in deep breaths. "Are you all right?" he asked.

She looked down at his strong hand, curved over hers, his tan skin a stark difference next to her lily-white. "I'll be fine. I just need to get there. Face things. I've had the nightmares for the past decade, and maybe just seeing things back to normal will help me get over whatever this anxiety is at the thought of home."

She squeezed his hand, hoping he would know how much it meant to her. Her teenage self would be squealing at the thought that Evan had held her hand without prompting, but the anxiety filling her trumped those thoughts, making it so she just had to breath and relax so she wouldn't pass out.

She could see the point of the mountain, the familiar sign that they would be at Silver Ridge Ranch within minutes.

And then from the ranch, it would lead on into the town and, eventually, to the spot where her home once sat.

"Almost there. I think Aiden and Taryn were flying in this morning, so they might already be there." Evan turned down the road that led to the family ranch, past the pond where they'd spent many summer mornings fishing. Then there were the stables for the numerous horses needed for tours as family reunions came to stay. The lodge loomed over them next, looking just like she remembered it, the large logs connecting at the corners and the three floors of guest rooms that stayed filled almost year round.

"It looks like they've got a group in for the festival," Evan said, pointing to the parking lot filled with cars.

They drove a little farther to the large two-story family home. It flooded Sadie with so many good memories that she struggled to fight back the tears. She didn't need Evan seeing her this vulnerable. He might have changed in some ways, but he probably wouldn't know what to do with a sobbing girl.

Evan parked the car and looked over at her. "Remember. Just say the word."

"Words. Corn dogs are two words, Goose." Her laugh relaxed her enough that she opened the door and stepped out of the Tahoe. The air was crisp and cool, causing her to rub her hands up and down her arms. She ran around the side of the vehicle and met up with Evan. "I forgot how cold it gets here. I've been in all the warm places this past year."

They were only a few steps away from the front stairs when the door opened. A woman with thick gray streaks in honey-colored hair came out, her hands over her mouth.

"Sadie-bug! Oh, girl, isn't this the best surprise ever! First, I get all of my kids to come around for the festival, and then I get the present of having you visit. Come here, girl, and give me a hug." The woman moved down the steps and met Sadie, wrapping her in a tight hug.

Sadie hugged back, feeling a couple of tears sliding out. "It's so good to see you, Dolores. The place looks as great as ever."

Dolores took a step back and used her thumbs to wipe at the tears rolling down Sadie's cheeks. "It's even better now that you're here." She turned to Evan and gave him a hug. "It's about time you made it back home. It's been a few months, and I was beginning to worry that your hotel had swallowed you whole."

Her comment caused Sadie to laugh out loud, and Evan turned, shaking his head. "I'm just trying to get this one all done, Mom. You know how much work I've put into it. Once I've got everyone trained, I'll be able to escape and come home more often."

Dolores turned and walked up the steps, waving them to follow her. "Right, and then you'll ask Roman to find you another fixer-upper hotel, and we won't see you again for another five years."

"Why does Roman sound familiar?" Sadie asked as they walked into the house. The smell of freshly baked bread and something sweet made her stomach grumble.

"Come in here, and we'll get you two some stew. Roman is one of Evan's frat brothers, the British one, I think." Dolores smiled as she scooped beef stew into two bowls.

Evan slid onto one of the stools at the bar and patted the one next to him for Sadie to sit down. For some reason, it felt intimate, like something he should be doing for a girlfriend. She sat, taking the bowl and turning her thoughts to her stomach and not how good he smelled next to her.

"Roman is an international real estate broker and developer. A lot of the guys from Delta Phi have tried to help each other out where we can with our businesses. He helps me find places that are more run down that I can renovate and then make a profit, like the hotel in Vegas. I've built a few hotels, but there's something about revitalizing something that's already built. As though it has a story but just needs a good shine." He stirred his soup around. "His fiancée, Isabelle, is a designer, and she came out for a couple of weeks at the end of August to help give tips for the décor."

"I'd been wondering who your designer was. I didn't think it would be all your ideas that could move in such cohesion." She giggled and elbowed him playfully.

He gave her a feigned look of hurt, and something about it—the whole day, really—seemed to settle her, like she could really have peace in her life. Sadie took a bite of the stew, savoring the flavors. It had been some time since she'd had a good home-cooked meal, the last one probably from this kitchen.

"Is Roman one of the members of the IBC, or whatever it is you call your little club?" Sadie asked, trying to hold back a grin.

Evan did the same and said, "Little club? How did you hear about our club?"

"Aubrey was laughing about it one day a while back. It sounds like you need to have a treehouse or something." She was able to hold off her laugh only long enough for Dolores to join in, and the two of them laughed while Evan just shook his head. "What does IBC stand for anyway?" she asked.

Looking as though he had swallowed a large chunk of meat, Evan took a second, pounding his fist against his chest.

Dolores finally spoke up. "It's International Billionaire Club. Aiden's a part of it too. It's still crazy to think that I have kids who've been able to turn a passion into a career, but I'm proud of all of them." She beamed, and Sadie thought of all the times Aubrey had felt guilty for her love of medicine. With Dolores's words, Sadie knew their mother was telling the truth.

"Where is Darren?" Evan asked, breaking off a piece of bread.

"He and the kids went into town to get some more rope. Some of the guests broke several cords of it, and we're trying to stock up for the weekend. There are a lot of families in town this year, and I'm excited to have my whole family to show off." She grabbed a rag from the sink and started wiping at the countertop. "Travis is flying in tomorrow morning, so we'll have the whole gang with us."

Sadie could see how excited Dolores was at the prospect of having her family together. With the oldest son, Darren, being the only one still on the ranch, it was probably hard to get the rest of her family together as they lived several hours or states away and were busy with their own businesses and dreams.

Carl Pearson, Evan's father, strolled in, setting his cowboy hat on a hook on the hall where Sadie could see. Walking in a bit farther, he stopped short when Dolores turned and said, "Don't be coming into my clean kitchen with boots that look like that."

With a sheepish grin, Carl turned and moved the few steps back to slip off his cowboy boots. With a quick shuffle step toward his wife, he gave her a kiss and said, "Do you mind scooping me up some stew while I wash my hands?"

Dolores gave him a look that said she was unsure she should do it, before moving to pull another bowl out of the cupboard. "How did the rides go?"

Sadie remembered going on a few excursions with some of the guests that stayed at the lodge. They would take several horses out on a trail that led back into the mountain behind them, allowing the people to experience an easy ride, especially since most of them had little to no experience with horses.

"They went well. Aiden and Taryn took the last group out about an hour ago, so we'll just have to keep an eye out for them." Carl leaned against the counter and scooped a spoonful of stew into his mouth. He looked up and stopped, blinking as if he weren't seeing clearly. "Hey, you two. I didn't know you were coming in."

"I'm surprised Taryn kept it a secret. She's the one who convinced Sadie to come home." Evan turned and gave her a smile, causing her insides to flip.

"Where's Aubrey?" Sadie asked, hoping to deflect any questions about why she'd stayed away for so long.

Dolores looked at Carl, who smiled and said, "I think she was out cleaning the stalls, grumbling about coming home and having to do the worst job."

Sadie and Evan both laughed. But it was Evan's comment that sent her into fits. "She's the youngest. She may as well get a taste of what the rest of us had to do."

Sadie tried to sober as she said, "Younger than you by two whole minutes. I'm sure that has made her life easier."

Dolores stuck out her hand, and Sadie gave her a high-five, the room alive with laughter. Sadie felt the happiness well up inside and thought about how different this home had been than her own. Things in her family had been mostly tense. She hadn't felt able to be herself or speak her mind until she'd gone to college.

"Well, eat up, you three. We've got a few more things to get ready before the festival starts in the morning. I'd love to say you could sleep in, but we'll be working from dawn 'til we drop tomorrow, so I hope you're prepared for it."

Sadie nodded when the woman pointed at her. "I'm kind of excited now. It's been so long since I made it to the Fall Festival."

Evan turned, talking in a loud whisper. "You won't be excited when you end up being the gopher tomorrow."

Dolores picked up the paper from the counter, folding it in half, and tried to swat at Evan, who jumped out of his chair and moved back before she could make contact. Turning to Sadie, she said, "I always had the hardest time catching him to give him a whooping. But I guess those reflexes were good for a lot of things. I'm just glad you decided not to go pro."

Evan resumed his seat, his mood more somber now than before. Sadie saw the muscles in his jaw tighten, much like they had after she'd said something to him about being arrogant back in college. That must be another soft spot.

She reached over and touched his hand on his knee, squeezing it a bit. He looked up at her, that same vulnerability in his eyes. She gave him a small smile, hoping he could understand that she'd be there for him too. Maybe the guy with the big ego wasn't as arrogant as she'd imagined.

CHAPTER 11

After sleeping in his old room with Aiden in the other twin bed next to him just like old times, Evan could hear his parents getting up early that next morning. Clicking on his phone, he saw it was only four in the morning and groaned, knowing he should get up and help. Every part of him was tired, and he hadn't even begun to do the regular work of the ranch.

"Aiden," he whispered. "You up?"

A groan came from the other side of the bed. "Do I have to be?"

"I thought we'd have a couple more hours of sleep, but I guess I forgot to factor in that we lost an hour when we crossed state lines."

Aiden rolled over as if trying to get comfortable again. A knock came at the door, and Evan held still, waiting to see who would break and get up to open it. They'd done that many times growing up, and Evan felt like he was in some weird time loop. After the knock came again, Evan threw back the covers and walked to the door, turning the handle.

"Huh?" he grunted as he tried to shield his eyes from the light in the hallway.

"We need to get going. Do you mind helping out with the cows this morning?" his father asked, his voice echoing down the halls. He'd never been able to whisper, and this early in the morning, it sounded like he had a speaker next to Evan's ear.

"I'll make Aiden do it."

From behind him, Aiden said, "You will not!"

His father grinned and shook his head. "You'd think the two of you would be grown up now. This sounds like the same argument we've had to mediate for twenty-nine years. Go get to the cows, now. We don't want your mother crying over wasted milk." He took off down the hall, his heavy steps echoing the whole way down.

"Come with me," he told Aiden. "Then maybe we can get a nap in before we have to go to the festival to help. I wonder why Mom and Dad are heading over there so early."

Aiden sat up, swinging his legs around to rest on the floor. "They said they couldn't get their booth to stand up on its own. Something about a board went missing. I bet Mom hasn't slept a wink, worrying about it."

"You're probably right about that." The booth the Pearson family put together every year was one of the most shopped, with options of fall and Christmas décor. From signs to hang on the front door to ornaments, his mother made them all and loved every minute of it. It helped that they also sold hot chocolate, an old family recipe that people had been trying to copy for years. Since the weather wasn't always reliable at the end of October, the warm liquid usually sold fast.

Working together, the boys finished with the cows by five thirty, enough time to head in for a quick nap before they had to get up at seven to head to the festival grounds. Even though the festival began on a Friday, there were already a lot of people in town for it, and when it officially opened at eight in the morning, there would be a large crowd waiting.

After a short nap and a quick shower, Evan came down the stairs for breakfast, dressed in his jeans and a plaid button-up. It felt a little strange to go back to this style when he was so used to wearing a suit and tie, but this was life in Aspen Hollow, and it was like slipping on a glove, preparing himself for the business of the day.

When he made it to the kitchen, he found Sadie and Aubrey already there, looking only half-awake. With a grin, he said, "Rough night? Or did you two just stay up late talking like always?"

"That is none of your business." Sadie's response made him laugh at the exaggeration in her tone, the corners of her mouth hesitating to turn upward.

Raising his hands in the air, he stepped over to the toaster to set a bagel in to toast. "I'm surprised you're already up, Aubs. I didn't even have to drag you out of bed."

"Please, I've been awake for the past half-hour. My legs are still hurting from cleaning out those stalls yesterday. I thought I was in shape with all of the working out and walking around the hospital all day." She reached up and rubbed her shoulder, her lips jutted out in a pout.

Evan let out a short laugh. "Ranch life. I think that's why it's twice as hard to stay in shape in the city."

"You and Aiden had to milk cows this morning, huh?" Sadie said, cutting a fried egg and placing a piece into her mouth.

Evan pulled out the cream cheese, grape jelly, and some milk from the fridge. "How'd you know about that?" he asked, turning to set everything on the island.

"I could hear you. You and Aiden aren't the quietest people in the world at four in the morning." One corner of her mouth turned up, causing Evan to laugh.

His bagel popped, and he pulled it out, setting it on a paper towel on the island. Spreading cream cheese and then a layer of grape jelly on top, he moved to pull a glass from the cabinet, filling it with milk.

"Ew. You still like that?" Sadie asked.

When Evan looked up, he saw Sadie's nose scrunched in disgust.

"Are you kidding? He's liked that since we were three. It just looks wrong." Aubrey made the same face as Sadie, and Evan laughed.

"Wow! I didn't know I could be insulted so much in five minutes. This happens to be delicious. You should try it." He held one half of it up to Sadie, who looked at it with suspicion.

After several seconds of what looked like internal debate, she leaned forward and took a bite. As he held it up for her, the move felt more intimate than he was used to, but after seeing the panic in her face when they'd driven closer and closer to Aspen Hollow, it felt right.

She chewed for a few seconds, her face neutral.

"Well?" he finally asked.

"It's actually kind of good. The flavors go together surprisingly well."

"That's what I thought. All you had to do was try it instead of knocking it all this time." He smiled at her, staring into her bright green eyes. As his gaze flicked down to her lips, for the first time in his life, he wished his sister would just disappear. What would it be like to kiss Sadie?

Once the thought entered his mind, his brain started backpedaling, reminding him of everything Stacey had done to him and that he needed to stay focused on getting the festival over with and then the wedding. Sadie's schedule didn't sound like she stayed in one place for too long, and for the foreseeable future, he'd be in Vegas, working to train his people at the hotel.

Footsteps sounded on the stairs, and Aiden appeared several moments later. "Did you put a bagel in for me?" he asked Evan.

Shaking his head, Evan said, "No, sorry, bro. I was educating Sadie on the finer things of life."

A light, airy laugh came from Sadie, and she put her hands up in a stopping motion. "I may have said that I liked the combination of toppings on the bagel, but I wouldn't go so far as to call them the finer things of life." All four of them laughed, and Evan dropped his mouth open, trying to make it look exaggerated. A moment later, he grinned, wiggling his eyebrows so she'd know he was kidding.

A few minutes later, the four of them headed out the door and piled into Evan's Tahoe. The other two scrambled into the back seat, leaving Sadie looking confused. She slid into the passenger seat, looking a bit stiffer than the day before.

Trying to shake it off, Evan pulled the vehicle out and onto the main road leading to town. It took a few minutes, and they sang along to the radio.

"Let's not start a band," Aubrey joked as the song ended. Her comment set off fits of laughter, and Evan sat back, realizing how much he loved this. He missed being able to pal around with these three and wished he'd realized that back in the day. Back when he thought football and being popular were the most important parts of high school.

"Penny for your thoughts," Sadie said.

He turned to see a serious expression on Sadie's face. Grinning, he said, "I just thought how nice it is to do this. It feels like old times with all of us together."

Her smile lit up her face. "It does, doesn't it? You looked like you were regretting something, though. Anything I can help you with?" She turned, and Evan saw Aiden and Aubrey engrossed in something on one of their phones.

"I was just thinking about how much I missed out on, especially in college."

"What do you mean? It sounds like most of your success comes from associating with your frat brothers."

Evan nodded. "True. I made some lifelong friendships. But your comment the other day made me realize that there were a lot of times when I didn't think about others or what they wanted. I just hope I haven't missed out on too many opportunities because I was too self-involved."

Lifting her chin, Sadie gave him a mischievous grin. "No time like the present to change that."

They pulled into what was normally a large field and piled out, the first rays of the sun shining over the horizon. Evan knew where to go on instinct, as the Pearson booth hadn't changed once in his lifetime. It looked as though his parents had gotten it to stand up, the several shelves and hooks in the back already holding several of his mother's crafts.

"You brought the whole gang," his mother said with a tired smile. "Okay, Aubrey, I'll need you to stay here with me. We'll be making trips to get more inventory out throughout the day. Aiden, I'll need you to help your father with the tractor train. Just help the kids get in and out, take tickets, etc." She paused, looking between Evan and Sadie before saying, "It's our year to be in charge of the kiddie games. Let's send the two of you over there."

Evan's insides jumped, excited at the chance for a little more one-on-one time with Sadie.

"Best to head over to Kiddieland right now, you two. I was able to set up some of the games, but there's still a lot to get ready, and we have less than an hour before the festival opens." Dolores smiled at them, and Evan took a step forward, Sadie following as they walked to the end of the festival.

"Do you know what they had planned for the kiddie games?" Sadie asked.

Evan shook his head. "I'm not sure, but probably the same thing they have every year. Bean bag toss, bobbing for apples, some kind of ring toss game."

As they made it to the area with the large wooden board painted to look like the candy house from Hansel and Gretel, he paused and waved Sadie through the shorter opening. Stepping through, Evan was surprised to find that someone had created a small village out of the usually open grassy field. Looking at all the options set up, he wondered why they hadn't had all this when he was a kid.

To the right, a section with small Nerf guns sat a few feet away from three large targets. To their left, the typical fishing pond was set up, with surprising detail on the curtain that hid the workers behind. In the back were the few games his mother had mentioned, and even farther back, they found a small race course and several small go-karts lined up and ready to ride.

"When did they start doing go-karts?" Evan grinned at the track, his eyes wide at the thought of what fun the go-karts would have been as a kid.

"I think Aubrey said Will has been working on them for the past few years," Sadie said. "I think this is the first time they've actually allowed them into the festival, though."

"Will Kennedy from high school? Wasn't he a couple years younger than us?" Evan pointed first at Sadie and then back at himself.

Sadie nodded. "He's taking over the mechanic shop now, I think. Dave was ready to retire."

Evan turned to look at her, his hand on his hip. "How do you know all of that? You haven't set foot in this town in years. I've been here for every festival since I was born, and I didn't even know all that."

With a sly grin, Sadie said, "It pays to listen. Your mom was talking about it last night, and I got curious about what people were up to."

"I'm guessing not that much has changed. Half of the people we went to high school with are still around, I'd wager."

"Oh yeah?" Sadie took a step forward, her head tilted up so she could see him. With the challenging look on her face, Evan was tempted to lean forward and kiss her, the temptation growing stronger as they spent more time together. This Sadie, so different from the girl in high school, had many more layers than he could have imagined, and that's what drew him to her.

"What if we take the go-karts for a ride? Just to make sure they're safe." Evan grinned at her and could see the indecision on her face.

She finally nodded. "Okay, but we need to drive for something. Loser buys ice cream from Kimball Farms."

"I thought they closed for the winter already."

"Nope. They're still open for the festival. But we'd have to get it by tomorrow." She held out her hand and looked him in the eye.

He reached his hand forward and shook hers, tempted to pull her closer, but she pulled away, heading for one of the karts.

Looking around, Evan saw they were in the clear. After pulling the cord behind the seat of Sadie's and then his own to start them, he jumped into his kart, buckled his seat belt, and tested some of the controls. Sadie drove up next to him, trying to give him an intimidating look before it turned into a wide smile.

"Are you ready for this, Gibson?" he asked.

"If you mean ready to beat you, then, yes, I am, Goose." She paused a moment and said, "Two laps around the track in one, two, hey—"

Evan punched the gas and took off around the first corner, going all of five miles per hour. The straightaway wasn't bad, but then came another curve, and Sadie came up on the outside and moved past him, her auburn hair flying behind her. The determination he saw on her face made him laugh, and he pushed the pedal down until it wouldn't go any further.

Moving up behind her, he tapped the back of her kart before moving over to the side. He hadn't realized there was another turn coming up as he'd only been focused on moving around Sadie. Swerving the best he could, the kart slid out and into the pile of tires stacked up for a barrier. The smell of rubber permeated his nose, and he realized there probably wasn't a reverse on these things.

He unbuckled his seat belt and moved his legs out, trying to get out of the smaller space. Once his feet hit the ground, he pushed up, inspecting the damage to the kart and the tires.

The sound of another kart pulled up behind him.

"Goose, what did you do?" Sadie asked in mock horror.

"Just come help me fix this, will you?" Evan glanced at his watch and saw they only had about fifteen minutes to get everything back to normal before the festival officially opened.

They picked up tire after tire, layering them so they would be more firm than just tall stacks of tires. By the time they'd finished, Evan could feel the sweat beading up on his forehead.

Sadie threw the last tire on the pile and dusted off her hands. As Evan looked down, he found they were both covered in streaks of black, and his hands were completely black.

"We look quite the sight, huh?" Sadie said, pulling her hair back and wrapping it in a band. As Evan looked closer, he saw a long black stripe across her cheek.

After wiping his thumb clean on his jeans, Evan reached up and rubbed it across the streak, the color wiping away. His first thought was the surprise at how soft her skin was, and then he was mesmerized in the bright green of her eyes. Something caught in his chest as he lowered his eyes to her lips, wondering what they would feel like on his.

Seconds passed, and just as he was about to lean in and kiss her, a voice behind him caused her to jump, as if they'd been caught doing something illegal. Which, looking down at the karts, they kind of had.

"Mrs. Dolores told us to come find you two over here. We're supposed to be helping with the games." He turned to find the owner of the voice, a girl about seventeen. With lips pursed and a hand on her hip, her expression told him she'd seen him try to kiss Sadie. Behind her were ten young men and women, their ages varying. "Where do you want us?" the tallest kid asked.

Sadie brushed back a loose strand of hair and said, "Okay, let's do two of you at each station. Who wants to be in charge of the go-karts?"

All eleven hands shot into the air, and Evan grinned. Sadie pointed to a young man in the back and a young girl on the other side. It took a few minutes, but she divided up all the kids, promising that they would rotate stations every so often to make it less boring.

"Are you ready? We are in charge of the fishing pond." She gave Evan a smile, and he nodded.

"That was very efficient of you."

"I've learned that in order to get everything ready for a

wedding, you have to give clear instructions to get things just the way you want them in a short time frame. You're the big businessman. Is that not how you do things?"

Evan considered that for a moment. "I've never really thought about it. But I'll definitely start doing that now. Maybe my remodels won't take forever and a day."

Sadie moved in the direction of the fishing pond, and Evan followed, his hand falling to the small of her back as they walked. It seemed like the most natural thing in the world, even though he hadn't escorted a woman to any event, even a fishing pond, in years.

The way she'd helped the kids get to where they needed to be was impressive. It felt as though another strand of rope had been cinched between the two of them, pulling him even closer to her. He just hoped it wasn't one-sided. He'd been through that before, and if he opened his heart again, it wouldn't survive much more heartache.

CHAPTER 12

They'd made it through the morning at the fishing pond, but Sadie still couldn't get the image out of her mind of Evan looking at her as he wiped away the black smudge. How many times had she imagined and daydreamed that he would finally notice her as a love interest instead of Aubrey's best friend? She couldn't even remember.

She'd thought she was over him, had moved on and locked her heart after college. And yet, it felt like those feelings had never really gone away and now were only getting stronger. Which meant she was just setting herself up for heartbreak.

A single life had been just fine, especially since she was able to make other people's wedding dreams come true. But seeing him, his carefree attitude and excitement for life, made her wonder what it would be like to have a relationship with him. Not that anything had changed from one lingering look, but she couldn't stop her mind from spinning it over and over.

Evan stood outside the sheet and would peek in every so often, telling her if the child participating in the fishing pond was a boy or a girl and about what age. They'd tried to switch at one point, but it seemed the age never made it through Evan's brain, as he usually gave kids either something too complex or too easy for their age.

"Girl, six years old," he said with a wink.

The line flew over the top of the sheet, and the clothespin came down enough for Sadie to clip on a small notebook set, which included a notebook, eraser, pencil, and pencil sharpener, all with the design of a unicorn. Whoever had thought of these gifts and toys must have blown the budget out of the water, because they were definitely nicer than anything she'd ever received in her years of coming to the festival.

The curtain on the other end opened, and Dolores came through, a bright smile on her face. "Aubrey and I came to give you a little break. You and Evan go get some food over at one of the stands."

"You don't want to eat? I think we'll be okay here," Sadie said, suddenly not wanting to leave her station. Things were going so well, and she worried that any change would suddenly burst that connection she felt between the two of them.

Dolores touched her arm, her eyes boring through Sadie's. "We've already eaten, dear. Go ahead and get something. We've still got a long day ahead, and I don't want you to get dehydrated or anything." There was something in her expression that Sadie couldn't put her finger on.

Shrugging, she moved past the curtain and saw Aubrey already taking over for Evan. He had his hands stuffed into his jeans and looked like he was waiting for her to come with him. The baseball cap on his head made him even more attractive at that moment, and she stared forward, willing her heart and brain to chill out a bit.

"What do you feel like?" Evan asked as they walked past the section of booths selling crafts and décor.

Sadie squinted a bit, trying to read all the signs along the row of food booths. The signs hadn't changed much, most of the same food being sold as in years past.

"Navajo taco," she finally said. "And a gallon of water." She hadn't realized how thirsty she'd become, but she was now glad Dolores had come over when she did.

Evan chuckled. "Yeah, water does sound good. Go find us a table, and I'll get the food."

Sadie reached into her pocket where she'd stashed some cash that morning, knowing she didn't want to carry her wallet around everywhere. Pulling out a ten-dollar bill, she said, "Here. This should cover my portion."

Evan shook his head and pushed her hand back. "I've got it. I'll be right back."

He moved away before she could protest, and as she watched him walk to the stand, she knew she was in big trouble.

CHAPTER 13

The picnic tables set up in the shade were packed with people, all trying to get food while listening to the band playing on the other side. Sadie could only find a small section on one end of the back tables, and she sat down, watching the people around her. It was something she'd done as a young girl, watching body language and facial expressions. She'd learned how to do that when she was really little, making her more sensitive to the feelings of the people around her.

A young mother sat just down the table from her, and Sadie smiled as the infant cooed and tried to attack the small toy sitting on the table in front of her. Sadie had always loved kids, had wanted a whole gaggle of them someday, but that was before she saw what her parents' marriage had dissolved into. Now that she wasn't planning to marry, ever, she didn't want to try to bring a child into the world without the help of someone she could depend on.

Her life would change considerably if she ever had children, but she was willing to do that—in dreams, that is. As much pull as she felt toward Evan right now, she knew it was probably all in her head, or even if it was real, it would fizzle out by the time they both had to go back to work and reality.

A plate of food slid in front of her, and Sadie scooted a little closer to an older woman she didn't recognize. Evan sat next to Sadie, and she realized just how little room they had.

"Sorry, there weren't many open seats." She gave him a sheepish look, and he only grinned.

"No worries. Do you want me to sit on the ground to give you more room?"

Sadie blinked a few times, surprised at his offer. The Evan she'd always known wouldn't have noticed or wouldn't have cared about something like that.

Part of her wanted him to, just so she could have the room to move her arms since she'd have to cut the scone with a fork and a knife. The other part of her caught the woodsy smell of his cologne, and with his arm right next to her, she didn't want him to move.

Shaking her head, she said, "You're good. I think these people next to us are almost done anyway." Seeing the warmth in his smile, Sadie averted her eyes to her plate, focusing on cutting into the fried dough. Her insides felt like they'd been shocked and were trying to recover.

She felt like a love-sick teenager around him, but she wished she could just push the feelings aside and move on. She had Taryn's wedding to finish preparing for and another four weeks after that. If she looked at her calendar, she'd be all over the country in the first few months of the next year, and how would that work with a relationship?

"How's the food?" Evan asked, stuffing a large bite of bratwurst and sauerkraut into his mouth.

"Delicious as always. I really need to pay you for it." She moved to reach into her pocket again, but he stopped her, placing his hand lightly on her arm and sending tingles throughout. She wished she could curse her nervous system for being so sensitive to his touch.

"Please, it's on me."

"But our bet was for ice cream, not a taco." Sadie tilted her head to the side and raised an eyebrow, challenging him to defy her.

Evan looked like he was trying to keep back a smile, and then he chuckled. "What if I want to buy you a taco and ice cream? I think that's allowed, don't you?"

"I do have a job. I can buy things."

"Why are you being so difficult about it? It was my treat for putting up with me all morning at the fishing pond. And for driving here with me. I know it was hard, but you seem to be having a lot of fun."

Sadie looked back to her food, thinking about that. "I am. Thank you. So far, no corn dogs have been needed. Speaking of corn dogs, how can you eat that," she asked, pointing to his bratwurst, "and not corn dogs?"

"I'm not really sure," he said, staring at the piece of meat on his fork. "One of the guys from the IBC is from Germany, and he knew how to cook them really well."

Lifting one side of her mouth, Sadie said, "I think it's from when we were in junior high. Remember, someone dared you to eat five of the lunchroom corn dogs?"

Evan's eyes widened, and he laughed. "I didn't even remember that until you said something. You know what? I think you're right about that. I went home feeling sick and ended up throwing them up. But I made twenty bucks, so I'd say it was worth it."

Sadie raised an eyebrow, not sure she'd feel the same. "Throwing up is not worth a hundred bucks."

They paused a few moments as the couple next to them moved. Sadie shifted over a few more inches, allowing Evan to scoot all the way onto the bench but close enough that she could still inhale his heavenly cologne.

"Do you have a boyfriend?" he asked, right as she took a sip of water.

Half spitting it out, half choking on it, Sadie felt her eyes water as she pounded her fist against her chest, trying to get everything to clear out. Evan patted her back a few times and moved his hand in circles, causing her to relax and focus on that rather than the tickle in her throat.

"Sorry, I didn't mean to startle you." Evan looked concerned, as though he were the one fully responsible for the burn in her chest. Which he kind of was.

"You're good," Sadie said, waving it off. "I, um, no. I don't have a boyfriend." She kept her eyes on her plate and breathed in slowly before letting it out in segments. Armed with the plastic fork and knife, she cut the scone, making sure the meat, lettuce, and other toppings were still atop it as she raised it to her mouth.

Evan took a sip from his water bottle and asked, "Have you had a boyfriend recently? Like, since college?"

At that, Sadie tipped her head back and laughed longer and louder than she had in a while. "That's funny."

"Why is that funny? It's a simple question."

"Well, I don't date as often as you do, Mr. Vegas." Sadie slapped her hand across her mouth, her eyes going wide as she realized what she'd said. She might have kept up with him for a few years, and most of the media liked to focus on celebrity couples or who they were dating, which made it easy for her to know.

He turned toward her, his elbow resting on the painted white table. "What is that supposed to mean?" He looked more curious than offended, and Sadie was grateful for that.

"I'm just saying that it seemed like after Stacey broke things off, you were seen with several women."

A slight smile drifted over his face, and he raised an eyebrow. Leaning a bit closer, his voice just above a whisper, he asked, "Have you been keeping track of me?"

Trying to keep her emotions from bubbling to the surface, she said, "I read magazines because it helps me come up with designs for weddings. You just happen to be in a lot of them."

The corners of his mouth ticked up. "I hate to break it to you, but those were not former relationships. Sometimes, they are last minute dates to functions I absolutely have to attend or models for a certain product I'm endorsing. I haven't had a relationship since…"

"Since Stacey?" Sadie whispered, moving her hand over his and squeezing it, much like he had when they'd driven close to town the day before.

He nodded, his jaw tense.

Waiting a moment to decide if she should ask the question playing in her brain, she decided it was better than always wondering. "Do you still love her?"

Evan's hazel eyes turned to hers, and for a moment, Sadie wanted to look away, wondering what the intensity in them was supposed to mean.

"No, I should have realized that we were different people than when we first dated in high school."

"Or the million times after."

Evan let out a low chuckle. "That sounds like it comes with a story."

Closing her eyes, Sadie wondered if she should say anything. She'd never told anyone she'd had a crush on him, not even Aubrey, although she suspected Aubrey knew.

"I just watched the two of you throughout high school and then off and on during college. I always wondered what you saw in her." Sadie felt the heat reach up her neck and burn in her cheeks.

Evan turned his gaze forward, biting his upper lip as he thought about something.

Sadie focused on cutting the last few pieces of her Navajo taco, giving him some space.

"I guess it was just easier. We'd been in a relationship so many times that I just thought it was how things were supposed to be. But I should have seen the signs before I even proposed. I was just ready to settle down and have kids." The muscle in his jaw pulsed, and Sadie studied his profile, feeling a mixture of pity and attraction that he was even admitting all of this to her.

"And now?"

"And now, what?" he asked, his tone curious.

"Do you still want to settle down and have kids?" Sadie could feel her heart pound, the sound of it reaching her ears.

He shook his head, his eyes searching her face. "Yeah, I'd love to get married and have a family of my own. Traveling is fun, but I always wish there was someone at my side who could come along with me. There are so many things I want to share with someone, but, well, there's a lot of doubt that goes into a long-term future now." He paused for another drink of water and then turned back to her. "What about you? Do you want kids?"

Sadie laughed, realizing she'd just had that mental discussion with herself before he'd brought over the food.

"I did once. I don't know if marriage is for me."

Evan balked at that. "What do you mean?"

"You don't know how bad the fights got between my parents. There were times when I would just go to your house after school and stay the night so I didn't have to hear what they were screaming about again."

Sadie's sight clouded, tears forming as she recalled several of the arguments her parents had over money or over time away from one another. She reached her finger up and wiped at a tear before it had time to roll down her cheek. Evan wrapped an arm around her shoulders and pulled her closer to him.

She sobbed a bit, trying to contain the tears as much as possible. After several minutes, she took a deep breath. "I'm sorry. Should we get back to our stations?"

"Are you sure you're okay?" Evan asked, concern written on his face.

Sadie laughed, the sound hollow to her own ears. "I'll be fine. It's just memories I've buried coming to the surface. Thank you for the food. I appreciate it."

They stood, taking their paper plates to the large garbage can at the corner of the section of tables.

"Head on over there. I'm going to run to the restroom for a minute." Sadie smiled at Evan, hoping to convince him that she'd be okay without him, but as he walked away, looking back once, Sadie knew she was treading in dangerous waters. What was she going to do about her growing attraction for her best friend's brother?

CHAPTER 14

Evan walked back to Kiddieland, his emotions churning within him. He'd never seen Sadie so hurt, the girl who'd always been so happy and carefree. He couldn't imagine what it would be like to have his parents fight that much, let alone scream at each other. They were far from perfect, but they usually got over any disagreement within a day or two. He was grateful for that at least.

The way Sadie had looked, with the tears in her eyes, had sparked something defensive within him. He wished he'd been able to see this side of her years before, to be there for her during the rough nights. He and Aiden had played plenty of tricks on Sadie and Aubrey during that time, and for them it had been all about having fun. But hopefully it had helped ease her discomfort when she'd stayed at their home.

As he continued through the festival grounds, he looked back once and saw her still watching him. He wondered if he should walk back and take her somewhere, let her talk about everything and anything she needed to. Her parents' divorce was years in the past, and she probably had already divulged everything with Aubrey. But some part of him now felt jealous, like he should be Sadie's confidante.

Maybe it was just the magic of this small town, but it seemed to be stripping away the pretense and helping him see Sadie for who she really was. He'd always wondered if she'd had a little crush on him when they were younger, and her avoidance of that fact made him smile. But the question was, did she feel the same way now? His feelings for her were growing by the day, but he wasn't sure it could work between them. It seemed they were both broken with their own problems.

Sadie met up with him a while later, her face flushed and looking as though she'd been crying more. He had the urge to pull her into his arms once again, to breathe in her vanilla scent and pretend like they could have a future together.

Aubrey went with Evan to the ring toss station, and when Evan recognized his disappointment, he knew his feelings for Sadie were deepening. He'd have to decide whether that was something he wanted or not, and then there were her feelings to consider. He wanted marriage, kids. If she didn't think she could do it, he wasn't going to force her. Not that they were at that point just yet, but Evan had an inkling.

"What's got you so distracted today?" Aubrey asked as she gathered up the rings from the last little kid who'd played. There wasn't a line waiting for them like at the fishing pond, which made him wish he was still with Sadie. He liked learning more about her past, and maybe, because he'd listened, her ideas about him being arrogant had changed somewhat.

Shaking his head, Evan glanced over at the fishing pond where Sadie was bent over, talking to a little girl. "Nothing."

Aubrey must have seen the direction in which he looked, because she took a seat on a foldout chair and said, "You should go for her."

Evan turned, eyebrow raised as he pretended not to know who she was talking about. "Who?"

With a quick fist to his shoulder, Aubrey laughed. "You know who, dope. Sadie. You two would be great together. She liked you in high school, but I think all the jerk moves you pulled in college turned her off."

"She told you that?"

Aubrey frowned. "She never told me she liked you, but I could tell. I do remember her being more vocal about her annoyance with you after that one party freshman year."

"I was a jerk. But I haven't had a drop of alcohol since Eddie's death. I'm just trying to figure out how to not be so arrogant anymore."

"Did she say that to your face?"

Evan licked his lips and nodded. "Yeah, the other day."

Aubrey touched his arm a few times. "And you didn't die?" she said in a mock tone.

Rolling his eyes, Evan growled. "Please, I'm not that bad, am I?"

"You've come a long way, brother. But really, give it a shot. You'll regret it if you don't try now."

"She said she doesn't want to get married."

"Are you already thinking that far ahead?" Aubrey's face was serious, and Evan tried to read his feelings.

"No, but I don't want to spend two years together and then have to start all over again. Not that she isn't a great girl, but if I'm going to get involved with someone, I'm done with heartbreaks. I just want it to be forever." Evan stared straight ahead, not wanting to see his sister's reaction.

Aubrey placed her hand on his arm. "You never know until you try. Just a few dates. See how it goes. If your gut tells you there's no chance she'll change her mind, then move on. She'll be planning a wedding in San Diego right after

Taryn's wedding, so maybe that will be enough of a separation to move on. But now's your chance."

Evan's eyes flicked back to Sadie, and she glanced in his direction. She gave him a small smile before turning back to the little girl in front of her. What would life be like with someone by his side? He'd have to figure that out.

CHAPTER 15

Friday afternoon and evening passed rather quickly, and Sadie found herself exhausted by the end of it. Evan drove her, Aubrey, Aiden, and one of the nephews back to the ranch house, and she had a hard time keeping her eyes open for the quick ride.

Saturday began much earlier, as Dolores had arranged a fitting with the local bridal shop, and they spent over two hours having Taryn try on dress after dress. There was nothing that seemed to stand out to the small crowd of ladies until the final dress was tried. All four of them teared up as Taryn said it was the one.

It was nearly nine by the time they made it to the festival grounds, and Carl looked like a lost puppy, unsure what to do without his wife's direction. Sadie didn't get a chance to work with Evan again until that afternoon. They were stationed at the family craft booth when Carl came over.

"I, uh, well, your mother…" he said, looking at Evan. "She told me that I need to take a turn back here. We need you two to drive the hay wagon." The way he was hemming and hawing, Sadie could tell something was up.

From the look of disbelief on Evan's face, she knew he saw it too. "You never give that job up. Why did she say we needed to do it?"

Carl opened his mouth and clamped it shut again. "She, um, didn't give me a reason. The next wagon leaves in about ten minutes, so best get over there. You remember the route, right, son?"

Evan chuckled and slapped his dad on the back. "After all this time, I think I've got it, Dad." Turning to Sadie, he said, "Let's head over. I think I can hear Mrs. Goodwyn complaining already." His wide smile sent her whole body humming with an excitement she hadn't felt since, well, since their near kiss the day before.

She hadn't been on a wagon ride since she was probably fourteen. Her family had never run a booth, so she'd usually helped Aubrey with the different booths the Pearson family was in charge of. In fact, she couldn't remember a time when both of her parents had attended at the same time.

Was that the secret to the Pearson family? They seemed so happy together and did a lot to help each other and the community. And it seemed like they got together as often as possible, even though four of their children lived out of state. Was that the bit of life advice her parents had missed out on? That doing things together makes a stronger relationship?

They walked in silence to the wagon, but it didn't feel awkward, for which Sadie was grateful. So many thoughts were spinning through her mind that she was surprised when they arrived at the horse-drawn wagon. Evan took her hand and helped her up into the wagon's driver seat before disappearing around the side.

She turned around and watched as he set down the stairs and helped everyone climb on. The smile on his face sent a shiver down her spine and through her toes, and she wondered if he enjoyed life back in Vegas or if he missed the ranch life. Since Darren had taken it over, there wouldn't be much for Evan to do, but he could always buy his own if he missed it that much. But the idea of doing that and it not being in Aspen Hollow was something she couldn't see him doing. As "city" as he came off, there was still a bit of small-town boy inside him.

After the wagon was loaded, he jumped up into the seat next to her and smiled. "You good?"

Sadie smiled wide, happiness spreading throughout her body. "Yep. Where are we heading, Goose?" She watched as he turned and tried not to smile at that, and she was grateful. As much as she wanted to let herself fall for him, she wasn't in a rush to do so, and keeping things in a teasing mood would help.

"I think Farmer Thompson's pumpkin patch. You think you can handle that?" He looked at her over his shoulder as he picked up the reins and urged the horses forward.

"Is that where it always went? I've been trying to remember the last time I went on this thing."

Evan shook his head. "No, it used to just make a loop around the town. But this is a way to let people pick up a last-minute pumpkin before Halloween."

Sadie studied him. He was wearing a different pair of jeans today and a white t-shirt but the same hat as the day before, only turned backward. For some reason, he was even more attractive that way, and she rolled her lips in and faced forward, hoping he wouldn't ask what she was thinking right then.

Her thoughts from earlier invaded again, and she asked, "Do you miss it here? Would you ever move back?"

He squinted his eyes and pinched his lips together in thought. "I've thought about it every once in a while. Maybe buying a home here and then just heading out to check on the hotels every once in a while. It would be nice to raise a family in Aspen Hollow, away from the bustling city, but maybe I'm just biased since this is where I grew up and learned how to work, and my family is still here."

"Well, not all of them. But you grew a lot at Hawthorne, right? That's definitely suburb-cityish."

He nodded slowly as if collecting his words before saying them. "True. But I think that had more to do with the guys in Delta Phi and Coach Montgomery more than actually being in the city. What about you? Where do you see yourself in ten years?"

The question seemed to echo inside of her, and she wasn't sure what to say. "Honestly, I haven't thought that far ahead. I think my sights are usually six months out, especially when I have a wedding that far in advance."

"Well, take a minute and think about it and let me know." He wiggled his eyebrows, trying to be funny, even though she saw nothing but a serious study of her.

Settling into the seat, she looked around her, the beauty of the colors of the leaves on the trees standing out against the pine trees in the mountains near the town. They passed a small field of cows grazing, and with the sun almost behind the hill in front of them, she felt at peace.

"I guess if I found a way to move past all of the night-mares, this wouldn't be a bad place to live. It's the memories that scare me, but would driving past my old house or the sites of other memories every day help me to get over that? I'm not sure. And then there's the idea of my wedding plan-ning business. As much as I love it, I'm scared to get too big. I like the anonymity I have right now, and I don't know if I could give that up."

Evan nodded, glancing at her every so often. "That's a lot to process. The great thing is you don't have to know it all right now. Looks like we're here." He stopped the horses and slid off the seat and held out his hand to her. "Do you want to get down?"

She smiled and placed her hand in his, feeling the warmth of it as well as the roughness of callouses. Whatever she'd thought before about him not having to work manual labor because of his billions, she realized she'd been wrong. She didn't know what he did to stay in shape, but when she stepped down, she stumbled right into his defined chest, removing all doubt about being fit. Her cheeks started to burn, and she stepped away, moving in the direction of the passengers.

Over the next thirty minutes, they waited as the twenty or so riders decided which pumpkin was right for them, some of them easy enough to carry while others were large enough to need Evan's help. Sadie walked around with the clippers, making it easier to free the pumpkins rather than twisting them off the vine.

The ride back was short, and the sky was darkening. The brisk air made Sadie realize she'd forgotten all about bringing a jacket. As she rubbed her hands up and down her arms, she felt the chill spill through her.

Evan kept the team moving while pulling something out from a hidden compartment in the back of the seat. A fleece blanket.

"Your mom packed this, huh?" Sadie asked.

With a quick shrug, Evan smiled. "Who knows? That woman does tend to be prepared for just about everything."

As Sadie unfolded it over her, she could see the faint goosebumps on Evan's uncovered arms. Since the blanket was small, she scooted closer, handing him the blanket to move over his lower body.

"You can use it if you're cold. I'll be okay until we get back."

"Your teeth are chattering right now, and we have

another ten minutes or so before we get back. Just put it over you and stop being stubborn."

They maneuvered the blanket so most of his arms were covered while still holding the reins, and Sadie scooted a little closer, trying to make it easier with no wasted blanket space. Being so close to his body heat was just another benefit.

The feel of his arm next to hers sent her back to high school when she would fantasize about what it would feel like to have his hand surrounding hers. As if reading her thoughts, he reached his hand over and grasped hers, not saying a word in the process.

Sadie froze, worried that if she moved too much, he'd let go and the magic of the moment would be gone. She'd have to face it that her old crush feelings were back with a vengeance with the fulfilling of many of those old dreams. But could she make a relationship work? Was it possible for a girl who came from a background like hers to have a happy relationship with someone?

If it was a possibility with anyone, it was Evan, who came from the most stable family she'd ever seen.

CHAPTER 16

*R*eaching over and taking Sadie's hand had been a big risk, but she didn't seem to object. He didn't think she'd be one to totally rebuff him, but she'd been firm earlier about her convictions to not marry.

After dropping off the riders and helping them transport their pumpkins to their various vehicles, Evan hopped back onto the wagon and looked over at Sadie.

"Do you want to go with me to take the wagon back? Or did you need to get back to the house?" He watched as she bit her lip, and the urge to lean over and kiss her was stronger than ever.

"How about I run and get us jackets before we do that? My arms feel like popsicles." She grinned and slid down, running out of sight. It wasn't long before she returned, holding out a zip-up jacket for him.

"I found this in your Tahoe. Looks like you are prepared as well." She giggled as she pulled on her Hawthorne football hoodie.

"I can't believe you still have that. Didn't I give that to you when we were in college?"

Sadie nodded. "I forgot a jacket, and we were heading to that outdoor concert freshman year. You offered me this one."

"And you never gave it back," he said, teasing in his voice.

"You were kind of a jerk after that. Well, let me rephrase that. You were a jerk before, but after that, you were a total jerk. I tried to avoid you as often as possible from that point, especially after that party, and I kept telling Aubrey to take it back to you, but she conveniently forgot every time."

Evan turned to her, regret filling him. "I didn't realize I'd hurt you that bad. I'm really sorry."

Sadie studied his face for several seconds before she placed the blanket over her legs and then his, almost as a sign that she'd forgiven him for that terrible night in college.

That memory was one of those he'd worked to block out after ten years. It had been several weeks after he'd lent her his sweatshirt when the football team had won a big rivalry game. They'd come back to campus to several large parties throughout the dorms. He remembered seeing Aubrey and Sadie at a party, but it had been a while since he'd focused on the words he'd uttered when he saw her wearing the sweatshirt again.

"Look, it's my sister and her jersey-chasing friend." Even though he'd been drunk at the time, he'd never forget the look on Sadie's face, as though she'd been slapped. She'd nodded and left the party with Aubrey running after her.

Even later, Evan had never found the right time to apologize to her. Later that night was when his frat brother Eddie had died in a head-on collision, and then days later, several of the guys got into trouble for destroying their hotel rooms a few hours away from campus on a "bonding trip."

"Thank you for apologizing," Sadie said, pulling him out of his thoughts.

"I shouldn't have been like that to you or anyone. One

reason why I quit drinking. I made the winning touchdown in our big spring game and felt like I was on top of the world. But then Eddie's accident messed with a lot of us. That was when we trashed the hotel."

Sadie looked at him with curiosity. "I never heard about the hotel. I just remember all of Delta Phi having a memorial for Eddie. Was anyone else in the car with him?"

Evan shook his head. "No, which was probably a good thing. A bunch of us in the IBC contribute to a fund in honor of him and the family killed in the other car. We found out later that the family had two children who weren't in the car at the time and had to be taken in by family members. We've put them through college, and they're both leading relatively normal lives now."

Her hand flew to her mouth. "I had no idea. Aubrey only ever got bits and pieces." She paused a moment and then asked, "So, what happened at the hotel?"

"Gabe found out that his longtime girlfriend had passed away from cancer. She hadn't wanted him to know the extent of it, so she kept it from him, saying she'd be okay. A bunch of us took him out to help him feel better and ended up breaking a large amount of hotel furniture. That's when Coach Montgomery was named as the house mentor. He made sure all of us who participated in the vandalism worked it off."

"What did you have to do?"

"I worked in the hotel we trashed. It was spring, so we just had practice for football. I'd drive up to the hotel and work for hours in the laundry, and then sometimes they had me working with the maids when we were shorthanded."

Sadie laughed. "I'm surprised you wanted to keep working in hotels when that was a punishment."

Evan shifted, sitting as close as he could to her while still focusing on the horses and the road. "I paid it off at the end of fall my sophomore year. Then an opening came up at the hotel closer to school, and I worked at the desk. I learned a lot of the ins and outs of how a hotel works. But you wouldn't have known all that because you avoided me." He looked over at her, trying to gauge her reaction.

"Like the plague," she said, grinning. "So is that how you got your big start in owning hotels?"

"Kind of. Since I got a full-ride scholarship for football—"

"Ugh. Really?" Sadie said, cutting him off. "Do you know how many times I've heard you say that?"

Evan frowned. "Okay, I wasn't trying to flaunt that fact right now. Just listen."

Sadie adjusted the blanket up higher, tucking it around the shoulder furthest from him. She turned and rolled her eyes to say her patience was thin.

"All I meant was that since I didn't have to pay for school, the money I earned after paying off the debt went into a savings account, and I started small with a fourplex apartment building. After that, I took out a large loan to cover my first hotel and all the renovations. When it made a profit, I moved on to the next one and the next."

"How many do you own total?"

Evan scrunched his face together, trying to remember. "Twenty. But half of them are higher caliber hotels and bring in the more well-known clients or ones that have a lot of money."

"So, is that what you worry about? The money?" Her tone sounded somewhat bitter, and Evan backpedaled a bit, realizing what he'd said.

"No, again, I'm sorry. What I meant is that there are different tiers of hotels. I'm hoping to earn a five-diamond award for the one in Vegas."

"What's that?" Sadie asked.

"It's one of the most prestigious awards for hotels. There

are a lot of inspections and things that need to be met, but I've only ever received a four-diamond award for one of the hotels in California. It would be nice to reach that new level."

Sadie looked as though she were thinking harder than normal. "I think I understand. It's like me hoping to get the wedding with Charleigh French. Just a stepping stone. I like having a goal for something. It makes me push harder."

"Exactly. That was one of the things I struggled with most after football was over. I had always been training to break rushing-yard records or speed up my running. After graduation, it took a while to figure out I needed to create my own goals to reach higher. So far, I've been able to accomplish all the things I've set my mind to. If you think that's arrogant, then—"

Her hand reached out and wrapped around his bicep. "I'm sorry for saying that. Please forgive me. I guess I was just judging from the outside. Now I get that you want to improve, to get better all the time, and I admire that."

He looked over and smiled at her, her features lit up by the rising moon. They pulled into Farmer Thompson's property, and Evan maneuvered the wagon to sit where he'd been instructed by his father. They sat still for several moments, Evan's insides screaming at him to kiss her.

Leaning forward, he was inches away from pressing his lips to hers, when lights flashed behind him and someone called out, "Evan? Sadie? Are you still here?"

Pulling back, Evan made eye contact with Sadie and couldn't decide what it was she was feeling. "I guess we'd better go."

Sadie's voice sounded a bit breathless as she said, "Yeah, I guess we should."

Evan slid down first and held out his hand for Sadie, helping her climb down. He folded the blanket as they walked toward the car. Opening the back door for Sadie on the passenger side, he made sure she got in and then closed the door with a soft click. Walking around the front, he glanced over as the driver's side window rolled down.

Aiden grinned at him. "Did we interrupt something?" His voice was low, and Evan was grateful for that much. He didn't want to make Sadie feel awkward.

"Maybe. Just drive us home." He climbed into the seat behind Aiden, next to Sadie, as Aubrey was occupying the passenger seat.

"I feel like I haven't seen you two since the festival began. Did you have fun?" Aubrey's voice was normal, but from the little he could see of her face, she had questions she was dying to ask. Evan shook his head, widening his eyes in the hopes that she wouldn't bring up anything right then. Never had he felt more like a kid in high school than that moment.

"It was a lot of fun. I'm surprised by how much fun I had." Sadie grinned, and Evan could see the faint whiteness of her teeth in the dim light.

Aiden turned the Tahoe around and drove down a street on the right. "We need to pick up something Mom forgot to grab from Mrs. Goodwyn."

Thinking nothing of it, Evan turned to look out the window, enjoying the sight of the fields in the darkness.

"Corn dogs." The words were spoken softly, and Evan turned to look in Sadie's direction, only seeing terror in her eyes. He scooted over, wrapping his arm around her.

"What's wrong?" he whispered, grateful his brother and sister were talking about something that had happened earlier at the festival. "Are you okay?"

Sadie shook her head against his chest, and Evan looked up, realizing the source of her terror. They were passing the site where her home used to stand. She hid her face against him, and he squinted, trying to see what remained of the house. The town had done it's best to clear the property of debris after the fire had taken hold. Although it wasn't completely burned in the fire, the untouched part of the house was on the top floor. The bottom had been deemed unsafe, and the council had it knocked down when the Gibsons left town. It was nothing more than a block of concrete now.

Evan was stroking Sadie's hair, trying to get her to calm down, when Aubrey turned around. "Sadie, are you okay?" She turned to look out the window, and her head swiveled back, shock and sadness on her face. "I'm so sorry."

Aiden turned for a quick second before focusing on the road ahead. "What's wrong?"

"We drove down the old road. Why didn't you think of it?" Aubrey asked, giving him a light punch in the shoulder.

"I'm sorry, Sadie," Aiden said. "I wasn't thinking. This is the fastest way to get to Mrs. Goodwyn's house."

Sadie's body was shaking, and Evan did all he could to comfort her. He held her until they'd made it past the house and down a few more houses to where they needed to stop.

When Aubrey opened the door and jumped out, Sadie looked up and wiped at her eyes, tucking a thick section of hair behind both ears. The light wasn't the best, but Evan could see shame on her face.

Leaning forward, he put his lips next to her ear. "You don't have to be ashamed. Just know I'm here." He gave her a small smile when he pulled back, and she nodded, rolling her lips in.

Aubrey got back in with a few glass plates, and they took off, the two in front talking about random things from the festival. Evan was grateful for that as it was to avoid making Sadie feel bad.

Once they arrived back at the ranch, Evan pulled Sadie aside while the other two walked into the house. It felt strange that Aubrey would leave, as she was usually the one to comfort or talk to Sadie about everything. Maybe she was just trying to push them together some more.

Evan put his hands on Sadie's shoulders and looked down so he could see into her eyes. "Are you okay?"

Sadie nodded. "Thank you for holding me. I didn't think it would hit me so hard."

"Do you need to see someone about it?" Evan had no idea what to do about things like this and figured if someone were trained to deal with anxiety or trauma, they might be a good person to talk to.

"I've seen a therapist on and off for several years. I'll give her a call on Monday." Sadie said.

He wasn't quite ready to head inside, and he wanted to make sure she was all right. "Do you want to sit on the swing out back? We've already got a blanket." He held up the small blanket they'd used to cuddle with in the wagon.

She grinned. "I'd like that."

Before Evan had the chance to slip his hand into hers, Sadie placed her warm hand into his, and a jolt of excitement shot through him.

They walked slowly around the side of the ranch house, the bright moon above making it easier to avoid the large rocks in their path. Once they'd settled into the large swing, Evan draped his arm around her shoulders, pulling her closer to him as if he could protect her from further pain.

But holding her, something inside *him* healed, as if he'd just needed her by his side to make all his past mistakes seem less permanent.

She turned in his arms, her eyes bright as the moon shone off them. "Thank you."

"For what?"

"For helping me get through this. For giving me the strength to move beyond my past, if only a few steps."

He wasn't sure what to say, wasn't sure he deserved such

gratitude. Instead of saying anything, he leaned forward, capturing her lips with his ever so lightly. The same shock from her touch rippled across his face, and he kissed her again, the taste of her lips just as sweet as he'd imagined.

Pulling back, he saw a blush creep up her cheeks as she gazed into his eyes. With his heart racing and his lungs doing their best to produce oxygen, he leaned back, his head tilted up to look at the stars above.

The silence between them stretched on, but he felt no need to spoil it with words. This weekend had been one of the best of his life, and he hoped that his deepening feelings for Sadie Gibson would be returned. He'd just have to take things one step at a time.

CHAPTER 17

The next morning, the Pearson family got up early once again to ready themselves for church. Sadie woke up thinking the night had ended as a wonderful dream after it had begun as the realization of all her nightmares. But she could still feel Evan's kiss on her lips, even better than she ever could have imagined.

She'd been grateful that Aubrey was asleep by the time she came back in. As much as she wanted to spill it all to her best friend, she wanted to keep it to herself a bit longer. The safety she'd felt in Evan's arms had made the night pass much more quickly than it would have if left to herself.

Entering the old chapel, Sadie felt a mixture of comfort and unease as she remembered all the times she'd come here. There had been times when things were going well with her family, and church was usually the only time when her parents went out together in public. It was all a show for the town, but Sadie, even now, could feel the stares of the people that Sunday after the fire, pity and disgust in their eyes as they looked at her and her sister.

Dolores ushered the family to what had been deemed

the "Pearson Pew," and they all squished in. At one point, Sadie wondered why she'd even come at all, the dread filling her.

As the pastor spoke, he talked of finding a way to let go of the past and move forward, speaking to her as if he knew exactly what she needed.

Once the service was over, Sadie moved outside, needing some fresh air after the stuffy room. Aubrey and Evan approached her, both looking fairly timid compared to their usual outgoing personalities.

"Are you ready to head back to Vegas?" Evan asked.

Sadie nodded. "Yes. I think that will be good so I can focus on the wedding again. I gave your mom those boxes so she can finish what I have in mind for a surprise for Taryn. I didn't think we'd be so busy with the festival."

"That's what happens when you're with the Pearsons." Aubrey grinned and wrapped her arms around Sadie's shoulders, pinning her arms against her sides.

Looking at her roommate and best friend, Sadie said, "I'll see you in a couple of weeks. You're heading back to California tomorrow?"

Aubrey nodded. "Yeah. I have the night shift tomorrow night, so we'll see how that goes after this weekend. Maybe I'll sleep all day today since the two of you are leaving. Then again, Darren asked for my help with something for Melissa, so we'll see if I get any sleep anyway."

Dolores and Carl approached them, Dolores giving her a big hug. "It was so good to see you, Sadie-bug. We'll see you soon, right? I'll get everything put together for what you need for the wedding."

Sadie grinned. "Thank you. I think it will be the best focal piece in any of the weddings I've ever done."

Evan opened the door without saying anything, waiting for Sadie to get in. After shutting the door, he climbed into the driver's seat and stuck the keys into the ignition. When he'd pulled out of the parking lot, Sadie turned to him.

"Will you take me past my house again?"

With trepidation on his face, he asked, "Are you sure?"

"Let's just do it. I want to see it in the daylight."

They didn't say anything as he drove down several familiar streets and finally onto the one she'd known as home for sixteen years of her life. As she saw the concrete, something in her twisted, changing what she'd thought for so long. The same memories came flooding back as they had the night before, but it seemed like looking at everything in a different light was helping her to not have a breakdown.

The home she'd had nightmares about for years was nothing but concrete and weeds. As she thought about it, there weren't that many happy memories to go along with the property anyway.

Feeling a hand on hers, she looked down and saw Evan's covering hers. He gave her a close-lipped smile and gently squeezed her hand.

"Thank you for this. I think it's time to move on like the pastor said."

"If you could build any house here, what would it look like?"

Sadie glanced over the property again. "A white two-story house with green shingles and a white picket fence all the way around."

Evan raised an eyebrow. "Like the house from *Anne of Green Gables*? Wasn't that what you and Aubrey always fantasized about?"

Letting out a laugh, Sadie said, "Maybe. It was one of our favorite movies, and it always stuck."

"If you were to live in that house, what would you see in ten years?"

Sadie closed her eyes, trying to focus on his question. "A

few kids chasing a dog around the yard. Daffodils in the garden out front."

"And an attractive man at your side?" He winked, sending Sadie into fits of laughter.

When she didn't say anything, Evan said, "What? You don't want a guy with a strong jaw and hazel eyes helping with the outdoor chores?"

As Sadie looked into Evan's eyes, she could see that part of him was serious. "Time will tell, I guess." Parts of the wall she'd constructed around her heart were falling and her opinion of marriage shifting, and in some ways, it was freeing.

Shaking his head, Evan laughed. "Do you want to stay longer?"

"No. Let's head back to Vegas. I have a wedding to finish planning."

CHAPTER 18

The drive back to Vegas was uneventful, but it was fun to chat with Sadie as they wound through the old roads and made it back to the interstate. Vegas seemed to be as busy as ever, maybe more so compared to the slower pace of Aspen Hollow.

They had dinner Tuesday night, and Evan couldn't remember the last time he'd laughed so hard. She was fitting into his life more easily than he thought possible, and he just hoped it continued.

Evan was at his desk Wednesday morning when his phone rang. Looking down, he saw it was Sadie.

"Hey…uh, how's it going?" he choked out. He'd almost said, *Hey, beautiful,* but he didn't want to scare her too much.

"Oh, you know, just planning Taryn's wedding and then making sure everything is on track for the wedding in San Diego around Christmas. I've never done two so close together, but at least most of the other one is ready to go. Did you finalize any of the events for the week of Thanksgiving?" Sadie's voice sounded winded, as though walking somewhere.

Evan pulled out the book, a sudden rush of air leaving him as he remembered he hadn't taken care of it. "I will do that today."

"Okay, let me know when you've got them confirmed so I can put it on the itinerary. Also, Taryn said she won't be able to make it this week here to Vegas. Can you come with me to do some taste testing tomorrow? I figure you'll be able to help, at least somewhat, with what she likes."

"If there's food involved, I'm in. Where are you now? We can go get some lunch." Evan twisted a pen sitting on the top of his desk, trying not to hold his breath for her answer.

A loud wind sounded through the phone and then softened when Sadie's voice came through. "Can I take a rain check on that? I'm away from the hotel right now, trying to get some supplies, and it's not going so well."

Evan grinned, picturing her face at that moment with her stubborn jaw stuck in the air and her foot tapping. "Sounds good." Another thought hit him, and he opened his mouth, hesitating to ask. "Hey, Sadie?"

"Yeah?"

"Are you going with anyone to the wedding?"

He heard a slight laugh, and then she said, "I'm the wedding planner. I don't usually have to worry about that."

His heart sank a bit, realizing how disappointed he was at the sound of that. He paused, trying to think of something to say to that, feeling the small rejection more than he wanted to.

"I'd love to dance a few songs with you, though. Would that work?" she asked.

And just like that, his hopes skyrocketed. "Yeah. That would be great."

When she spoke, he heard a smile in her voice. "Awesome. Okay, I'll get everything set up for a tasting tomorrow. Do you mind if they come to the hotel? I think it will be easier and faster for me to have everything there. We're down to three weeks, and I have so much to get done before the big day."

"Yeah, no problem. That will help me get some work done as well. I've had a lot of calls come in for events the past couple of days, and I'm a little behind on my regular work."

They chatted for a few minutes and then hung up, Evan feeling better than he had in a long time. He wasn't sure where this would lead, but he hoped he could enjoy his time with Sadie and see where his feelings took him.

* * *

SADIE FELT ALL the tingles even the next day when she thought about Evan asking her to go to the wedding with him. She hoped he wouldn't feel too awkward showing up to his sister's wedding alone, but she couldn't commit fully to the evening by his side because of everything she'd have to coordinate. It just wasn't fair to him or her, but she was grateful he'd accepted the dances.

The next afternoon, she sat at the conference table, taking inventory of everything that had just come in that morning, trying to figure out what she still needed. The biggest thing was to nail down the catering in order to give the company enough time to pull it off. Feeling the pressure, a tiny part of her wished she had stayed in Vegas instead of going to the festival a week ago. So much of that time could have been used to get that much closer to finalizing the wedding.

But as she thought about it more, the trip had given her the chance to see another side of Evan. He definitely wasn't all arrogance and perfection, and she liked that about him. She appreciated his willingness to open her door and to help her feel comfortable when things got harder. Could she see herself with him long-term? She nodded, even though she was in the room by herself.

Did that scare her? Even more than anything she could have dreamed. She'd written off men for so long that she wasn't sure she'd know what to do in a relationship. But then again, she had a lot of stories from her past clients, which made things seem a little easier.

Looking at the time on her phone, she saw it was one in the afternoon. She picked up several papers and a folder, sticking her phone in her back pocket before leaving the room. She'd arranged for the catering company to meet them in the large area near the kitchen where cooking classes were sometimes held. It would give them enough space to quickly go through the options and decide which ones would work for the dinner and reception.

Just as she passed the elevator, the doors opened. Evan walked out, looking handsome in a bright blue polo shirt and navy slacks. He walked forward and gave her a hug, one that extended longer than normal, causing a current of electricity to whiz up her back.

When he pulled back, he asked, "Are you sure you need me for the tasting?" She focused on his eyes and saw pleading there.

Sadie stopped and studied his face, wondering why he looked like a caged animal. "It would help me go through the options a bit quicker. I need to nail it all down today so I can move on to the rest of the wedding." All the excitement she'd felt at his embrace disappeared.

He held her hand softly with one hand and glanced at the large watch on his other wrist. "I need to meet with one of the subcontractors at three. Do you think we would be done by then?"

With a shrug, Sadie said, "I'm not sure, but I hope so. The caterers should be set up so we can go through it all quickly.

If you don't have time, just say the word. I know how busy you are being hotel owner and events coordinator." She tried to make the comment light, hoping it would ease the tension in her chest.

She watched as he took a deep breath and nodded. "No, I should be fine. I'll stay as long as I can." He still looked like he was ready to bolt at the first sign of something, but what that was, she wasn't sure.

Sadie led him toward the kitchen, biting her bottom lip as she tried to figure out the sudden mood change. She didn't say a word, too frustrated by the whole event and berating herself for even thinking that a kiss and a couple of dinners would merit something more in their relationship.

"How are the wedding plans coming along?" Evan asked, looking somewhat distracted.

"Making progress. This is the major piece still needing to be figured out, and the rest is putting together decorations and making sure everything is lined up for the big day." She opened the door to the kitchen and held it for him, letting go once he stretched his arm out.

Winding through the kitchen, she saw the caterer had laid everything out over several of the workstations, and for once, she was grateful, hoping they could get this done quickly.

What was her deal? She'd always been professional, hadn't worried about getting her feelings all tangled up during a wedding. But here she was, getting hot and cold signals from the man she was falling in love with, and that didn't sit well with her.

She did her best to calm down, reminding herself that Evan had a lot of responsibility when it came to the hotel. If he was meeting with a subcontractor, that meant there was progress being made in the event room. And right now, the happiness of her bride was worth the pressure.

Walking into the large room used for cooking classes, she smiled as she saw a familiar man dressed in his white chef coat placing the last few plates onto the countertops.

"Ah, Tom. It's so nice to see you again." Sadie dropped Evan's hand to reach out to the man in the white chef coat. He took it, shaking her hand warmly. She'd done three other weddings in Las Vegas in the past few years, and she always used Tom as he knew what she wanted, was reliable, and gave the best quality she could ask for. If she could afford to hire him full-time and bring him to each and every wedding, she would.

"Miss Sadie, it's so good to see you again," he said, the trace of an Italian accent coming through. "I've brought everything from our menu for the bride to taste. But all I see is the groom. Do you still want to do this today?"

Sadie turned to look at Evan, who pasted on a half-hearted smile. "Actually, Evan is the brother of the bride. We are the stand-ins today to get this all taken care of."

Tom smiled. "Perfect. I know you are on a tight schedule, so let's get started." He waved them over to the first workstation, loaded with what looked like starters. A regular house salad, an antipasti, and several types of rolls sat atop it. Sadie reached forward and pulled a garlic knot from the basket, savoring the flavors. She'd missed these.

Evan stood next to her, looking at the food as though it were foreign or it would hurt him in some way. Leaning over, he asked, "You've worked with Tom before?"

Sadie nodded. "I've had a few weddings here in Vegas. He's one of the best caterers I've found. The quality is always spectacular."

"Good to know. I could use someone reliable we can call to cater events." Evan grinned at her, pulling a roll from the bowl and taking a large bite. Sadie watched as his grin widened and he nodded. "This is really good."

They moved over to the next workstation where a number of entrees sat: pastas, breaded meats, and several bowls of vegetables. Over the next hour, they tried pieces of each dish, and although Evan did a good job in giving his thoughts about whether or not Taryn and Travis would like it for their wedding, he was distracted and fidgety.

The final round was dessert. Seven cakes sat on the table, some of them covered in flowers and others were simpler with delicate embossing. In front of them were several slices of cake, and Sadie was excited to try them out. She'd never done a cake testing before, as most of the brides and grooms were able to do that part themselves. This would be quite the experience.

Glancing at Evan, she saw his stiff posture and the glazed look in his eyes. She reached over, squeezing his hand with her own until he looked in her direction.

"Are you okay?" she whispered as Tom was turned, getting something from a shelf in back.

His gaze turned to her, and it took a moment for him to blink, bringing him back to the present. "Yes, sorry. I've just got a lot going on. What did I miss?"

Tom placed two forks in front of them, gesturing to the cake.

Sadie picked up the silverware and handed one fork to Evan. He moved like a robot, that same glazed look return-ing. Something was off and she had a feeling it wasn't really about work. He'd never been like this before, but maybe the pressure was getting to him all of a sudden. She knew she was falling for Evan Pearson, she just hoped that he'd go back to acting normal after this day was over.

CHAPTER 19

Evan had actually enjoyed taste testing the menu with Sadie, and he found Tom's food to be some of the best he'd tasted in a while. He'd have to get the man's information to sway him to come work at the hotel for him, even if it was only for events.

The part he'd been dreading most was the last table filled with cakes of different sizes and colors. He'd thought about what taste testing food would mean after he got off the phone with Sadie the night before, and it had seemed easy enough—until it came to the cakes. He'd noticed the separate table for the frosted desserts from the moment he'd walked into the room. His stomach churned, memories of his time with Stacey as they planned their wedding surfaced.

"I've brought several cakes for you to try today," Tom began, waving his hands in front of the display. "We have some other options if this isn't what you think the bride and groom would enjoy."

Sadie smiled at his eager-to-please personality. "I think we'll be okay, Tom. They all look amazing."

Evan glanced over at her, but she wouldn't look at him,

her posture stiff. Trying to focus, he knew he'd have to talk to her after. He just wasn't sure how to explain that all of this was hitting too close to home.

"This first cake is a chocolate raspberry truffle, and it's filled with a dark chocolate ganache. Next is a salted caramel cake, which is a popular favorite right now." He waved for them to taste each piece.

Evan watched as Sadie sliced off a small bite of both with the side of her fork. He reached in and tasted each. The flavors were delicious, but the chocolate was a little overpowering for his taste.

"Next, we have a vanilla cake with an almond buttercream frosting. Beside it is a lemon berry cake, layered with strawberries, raspberries, and cream." Sadie again moved to cut a piece, but Evan could only stare at the yellow cake, his heart pounding in his ears.

That was the cake that was supposed to signal his forever life. He and Stacey had a hard time deciding on what flavor to get, as they had very different tastes in desserts. But after several occasions of trying new kinds, that had been the one they'd settled on, even down to the layer of berries.

He hadn't moved forward, still frozen when Sadie turned to him. With a loud whisper, she asked, "Are you okay?" She'd said it several times throughout the tasting but the memory overload was hitting him harder than he'd imagined.

"Corn dogs." His words were so soft, he wondered if he'd actually said them out loud. Feeling like a robot, he set the fork down on the table and said, "I've got to take this call." Pulling his phone out of his pocket, he swiped as if answering a real call and moved in the direction of the back stairs. He placed it to his ear and said, "Hello, Evan Pearson."

When he was out of earshot, he lowered the phone from his ear, his breathing so rapid that he became light-headed. It had been five years. Why was he still reacting like this?

As he sat on the cement stairs, he rubbed at his temples, hoping a searing headache wouldn't form from the dull one there now. As he sifted through his emotions, he realized that had he read the signs long before he'd gotten to the stage of planning his own wedding, he could have saved himself from heartbreak. But that was in the past. He needed to find a way to get through it, for his sister's sake, as well as for his own future.

Maybe it was better he'd had to help with the wedding as much as he had so he could work through all of this. What would he have been like for his second-chance wedding? If he ever got one, that is.

I'm sorry. Can we talk later?

He sent the text to Sadie, hoping she wouldn't feel like he'd abandoned her.

His breathing evening out, he trekked up the stairs to the second floor. He'd escape through the elevator there so he wouldn't have to face Sadie again today. She deserved an explanation of his abrupt behavior, and he would give it to her, but he still needed time to sort out his feelings. The last thing he wanted to do was hurt her, especially after all she'd been through, and he hoped a little time alone would help him get back to normal.

SADIE WATCHED as Evan retreated through one of the doors, pretending to answer the phone. She'd seen the blank screen as he pulled it out of his pocket. Whatever was going on with him, she wished he'd figure it out or at least talk to her about it.

After trying out the last few cakes, she tried to think of what Taryn would want. "Let's go with the fresh strawberries and cream cake. I'll send you a sample of the colors of the wedding so you can craft the flowers on it to match."

"Sounds good, Miss Sadie. It's a pleasure working with you again." Tom reached out and took her hand, shaking it lightly. He leaned in a bit and said, "It's probably a good thing you're not marrying him. He's the kind that would get cold feet, I think. I didn't have any corn dogs on the table, so I'm not sure why he would mention them."

Sadie pasted on a smile and said goodbye before heading back out the direction she'd come earlier in the afternoon. Corn dogs? Had Evan said that? Tom's words echoed in her mind, and it clicked in her mind that maybe Evan was dealing with the emotions of the past. She had no idea what it was like to be left at the altar, but she could imagine the littlest wedding decision could trigger some sort of memory for him.

Why hadn't she heard him say their secret phrase? Then she wouldn't have to search the entire hotel for him. She had been so caught up in worrying about how strange he was acting and wondering how he felt about her that she must have missed his cry for help.

She moved out of the room and in the direction of his office, hoping he'd gone there to hide out. The gym was the next place she looked, as he always seemed to head there when he had something on his mind. The last resort was his room, but as she got in, the elevator wouldn't let her go to the penthouse because she didn't have the card to swipe on the reader.

The text message lit up her screen and she felt the sinking feeling that she'd let him down.

Dialing his number, she willed him to pick up, hoping she could somehow give him the comfort he'd offered her in Aspen Hollow. It went to voicemail after several rings.

"Evan, I was trying to get to you, but I don't have access to your apartment. Just let me up so we can talk. I'm so sorry. Tom mentioned that you said our phrase, and I must not have heard it. I should have thought it through and realized how going through tasting cakes would make you feel. Just… call me, will you?" She paused for a few seconds before hanging up.

She'd give him the benefit of the doubt, but she was going to make sure she remembered her goals. She didn't need a repeat of that party in college again.

CHAPTER 20

*E*van took the elevator to his penthouse suite, not wanting to return to the office right then. Anything he needed to get done he could do on his computer or by making calls on his cell phone, and the thought of being stuck in his office felt suffocating. He received a text from the contractor saying it would be another hour before he could meet, opening up Evan's schedule a bit more.

He had seen a bit of concern in Sadie's features throughout the afternoon, and he felt bad that he'd been so aloof, but he couldn't help it. He wished he hadn't agreed to help her with the tasting, but he hadn't realized how many memories and emotions it would trigger.

Instead of working on the long list he needed to get done, with his phone on silent, he lay down, hoping that a few moments of relaxation would help him skip the dark hole he could feel himself slipping into. The thoughts of failure were overwhelming, and it paralyzed him.

He'd realized Stacey wasn't the one for him a few months after she'd left him at the altar, but that still didn't take away the feelings he'd had as they'd been planning the wedding. He remembered going to a tasting months before their wedding to pick the menu and how much fun they'd had as they joked about who would love the food and who would end up hating their choices.

It wasn't so much regret that he was feeling now. It was that loss of the future he'd thought he'd secured once he proposed to Stacey. After seeing Darren and his family at the ranch the week before, he realized how much he wanted that future to be real, and it left a deep ache in his chest. He wasn't sure how he could get rid of it, but finding someone to share a life with could be a start.

The only problem was, the person he wanted to be with didn't want a relationship at all. Was there some way to convince Sadie he wouldn't do to her what her parents had done to each other?

He still wasn't exactly sure how bad it had gotten with her parents, but her stories of the house fire told him there were more layers to her past. Sadie was so strong in every other aspect, but when it came to anything about relationships or talking about her parents and sister, she seemed to curl into herself, making it difficult to know how to help her.

Should he just not worry about her, let her finish out the wedding and then move on? What he liked about her was the fact that she didn't treat him any different because he had money, didn't fling herself at him around every turn. In fact, she'd been the only one besides his family to call him out on his behavior since...well, ever.

He had to admit he'd used his good looks to get out of a lot over the years, but that seemed to not have an effect on her. She would be the one who could help him be a better person, better boyfriend, and better man overall. She was worth the risk; he just had to push back all the memories of planning his own wedding and survive long enough to tell her and show her he was worth it.

After half an hour, he made his way out to his desk. Work was usually the best way to keep himself going, and maybe getting lost in it would help him forget his failures. He kept thinking about that five-diamond award because, in his mind, that would be the ultimate win to help reconcile all his past mistakes.

His phone lit up next to him on the couch, and he looked over, seeing Roman's name flash across his screen.

"Hey, man. What are you up to? Isn't it really late there?" Evan's clock on the wall across from him said four in the afternoon, meaning it had to be around midnight in England.

"Sleep is overrated." Roman chuckled. "How are things there? Everything going well with the hotel?"

Evan thought about the layers of plastic and paper all over the rooms on the first floor and chuckled. "Remodeling is still happening, but things are going well. My older sister, Taryn, is getting married here in about two weeks, so I'm pushing the guys to finish up so it doesn't smell like paint when she says 'I do.'"

"That's probably a good thing. You don't want her to grumble about that the rest of her life. I'm just calling about the retreat. Are you still in to have it over Christmas here in London?"

"What are you talking about? I thought everyone was coming here for it. I've got the space for everyone."

The other line paused, and Roman finally said, "I'm just kidding, bro. I've been talking to Jackson and Tristan, and they thought maybe we should do a beach retreat. Those of us with girls could bring them, and they could hang out while we talk business."

Evan's mind flicked to Sadie. As much as he wished he

could call her his girl, they weren't at that point yet, although a guy could hope.

"I could use a beach vacation. Let me know if you need help planning, and we'll go from there. Let's make it for the day after Christmas, though. My family will die if Aiden and I are both gone."

"True. I hadn't thought of that. I was actually thinking about doing something the week after New Years as an alternative if people can't make it. I know things get crazy, but winter is slower for real estate anyway."

Evan tried to remember if he had anything planned for that time. "That works for me. I should have my staff here trained, so I can take some time off. I'll just be traveling to check on the other hotels on the way back, so I'm game." He paused a moment and said, "How's married life?"

Roman scoffed. "We're engaged, not married, man. I'm hoping this wedding planning ends soon. I'd like a date where we aren't discussing some aspect of what we should have at the reception and what everyone will wear."

"When's the big day?"

"February. You'd better be here."

After pausing for a moment, Evan asked, "Roman, was it worth it? Taking a chance on Isabelle?"

Without a moment's hesitation, he said, "Absolutely. She's a designer, so I get why she's so wrapped up in the wedding. But I know it will end, and it will just be the beginning of our lives together. I can't wait for that point."

The ache in Evan's chest seemed to break into a chasm, and he rubbed it, as if that would help.

"I'm happy for you, man. Let me know the final decision so I can get dates scheduled on the calendar."

Hanging up the phone, Evan stared out the large windows in front of him, seeing several other hotels down the Vegas Strip. He'd done a lot to get to where he was as a billionaire at the age of twenty-nine, but the rest of his life had suffered. Then again, if Stacey hadn't broken up with him, he might not have pushed so hard, trying to compensate for the loss. But he couldn't go back and change the past, so he may as well look forward to the future, hoping Sadie would give him that chance for a do-over.

CHAPTER 21

Sadie spent the next week holed up in her room with a sewing machine she'd borrowed from one of the maids, crafting the last few things for the décor. Evan had been kind enough to bring her food or even send it up, keeping her company from time to time as she worked to get things done. He'd apologized for leaving the taste testing so abruptly but hadn't offered the complete explanation, which she could understand now that she'd figured out his anxiety. He hadn't returned to how he'd been at the ranch, but it was probably for the best, as she had so much on her plate to get done. At least he'd been grateful for her voicemail.

Thursday morning, Sadie took inventory of everything she'd received or made, trying to make a plan for what needed to be done in order of importance. The wedding was scheduled for the following Wednesday, the day before Thanksgiving, and as much as she'd accomplished, there was still a lot to finish before the big day. She'd checked off almost everything Taryn wanted on the list, when she got a call from the bride-to-be.

"Hey, Taryn. How is your fitness conference going?" Sadie

knew Taryn was asked to present at events often before this whole ordeal, but she was surprised just how often Taryn was in a completely different state when Sadie talked to the girl, crisscrossing the country from one day to the next.

"It's going really well. I'm in Charlotte for a few days, and then I'll be back out there. I'm so sorry I haven't been there as much to go through things."

"How about we do a video call, and I show you everything I've put together so far." Changing the call over to video, she smiled and waved at Taryn before turning the screen and pointing it at the array of things cluttering up the suite. She'd never been more grateful to Evan than in the past few days as she stumbled over boxes and other things in her wake. There was no way she would have survived in a smaller room for this amount of time with dozens of boxes. She'd already filled up a good section of the conference room.

As she walked Taryn through the lace accents she'd come up with, showing her some of what she'd been sewing throughout the past few days, Taryn would gasp and say, "Oh, that's beautiful," or, "Wow, it's amazing to see it come to life." With each *ooh* and *ah*, Sadie felt more and more confident as her planning skills proved to be on pointe with her client's wants and needs.

Until it came time to talk about the centerpieces and different signs throughout. Sadie had thought of using clear vases on the tables and filling them with a large bouquet of flowers, but that didn't sit well with Taryn.

"I'm sorry, Sadie, but I want people to be able to talk to each other across the table, not have to duck and bend over just to speak with someone four feet away from them. And I want the décor to be more rustic. I'll send you some pins I've found of things I loved, but I'm thinking something like an old wood planter box filled with mason jars and small bouquets of flowers. Maybe even a picture of Travis and me on the table. I don't want them to feel like this is way over the top, but rather a simple family wedding."

Sadie's eyebrow went up as she turned the camera back to her face. "Why didn't you have it at the ranch, then?" She hoped Taryn didn't hear the bite in her voice, the stubbornness in her coming out at being told that she, in fact, hadn't gotten all the details correct.

"With the extended families on both sides, we wouldn't have been able to house everyone. You know what the hotel in Aspen Hollow is like, and my parents can only hold about fifty or so guests in the lodge. It probably would have held a third of our guests. And while they could stay in St. George, we want them to feel comfortable and not have to drive so far just for little activities we've planned."

The logic was sound, but Sadie knew she'd have to do a lot of last-minute switching. Where was she going to find a place to make and deliver planter boxes? And if Taryn wanted something like that on the table, she'd have to incorporate so much more of the reused wood throughout the wedding. Ideas started flowing into her mind, only causing her chest to tighten. With a little more than a week left before the wedding, she was going to have to call in every favor she'd ever stocked up to pull this off.

As she hung up the phone with Taryn, she remembered Charleigh French and her description of the perfect wedding for her. They'd mailed an invitation to her, and Sadie knew this wasn't going to up her faith in Sadie's work. The vision she'd created for the perfect wedding for her best friend's sister that would also wow the celebrity was now crumbling down, as was the time left until the big day.

A headache formed behind her eyes, and Sadie laid her head on the back of the couch, hoping to keep it from turning into a migraine. That was all she needed. To be down during one of the most critical moments of her career.

When a knock sounded on the door, she wondered if she'd just been hearing things as it was so soft. But then it came again, a little louder. The great debate of whether or not she should answer it took off in her mind, and in the end, curiosity won. She stood, holding her forehead with one hand, and opened the door.

Evan stood there, dressed in dark jeans and a green t-shirt, his hat on, making Sadie grip the casing around the door, even with her eyes barely open.

"Are you all right?" Concern laced his face, and he placed his hand on hers over her forehead. "What's wrong?"

"I just have a headache. Come in for a second. While I'm up, I'd better get some ibuprofen in me. Otherwise, I'll be seeing stars." She moved to the bedroom and pulled out the bottle she kept in her purse. Letting out a few of the pills, she threw them back and swallowed, hoping that would be enough.

Evan stood in the entry, looking around with eyes wide. "Do you need anything else to help it go away? You get migraines a lot, if I remember right."

Sadie's stomach flipped with excitement that he could remember something as small as that, but she kept her wits about her, trying not to look like a lovesick teenager as she moved back to the couch. She needed to keep her heart locked up because she was already sick of the whiplash she was getting from the signals he kept sending.

"I should be all right for now. Time will tell." She closed her eyes and asked, "What's up?"

"I have to head to California tomorrow morning and wanted to make sure you were doing okay. I'll be gone until Monday, but I've alerted my staff to make sure you have everything you need. Speaking of which, do you want to put some of this up in my apartment?" He gestured to the boxes and things around the room.

"That would be nice, thank you. It's getting harder and harder to work in here with all of it, and I've already taken up the conference room downstairs."

Evan smiled. "Okay, I'll have someone come up and take it this evening. Anything else I can help you with?"

Laughing, Sadie said, "Do you know of anyone who is good with wood?"

"Huh?" He leaned closer, and Sadie grinned at him.

"Your sister has requested some last-minute changes to the décor, and I need someone who can make about fifteen planter boxes out of recycled wood."

Evan frowned. "She didn't tell you that a month ago?"

"I remember her saying rustic, but from everything she'd clipped to her wedding board, it wasn't quite to this extent. That was probably my fault that I didn't check on it." Sadie groaned. She was going to have to go without sleep for as long as possible to get it all done.

"What are you going to do?" Evan asked, taking a seat next to her on the couch.

"I don't know yet." The smell of him drew her in, and she moved, leaning her head on his shoulder. He seemed to stiffen for a moment, and Sadie wondered if she should move back. But he finally relaxed, moving his arm around her shoulder. She just wished they could stay like that for a while, not worrying about work or about some new décor she hadn't planned on.

"I'll see what I can do," he offered. "Maybe someone can make them in time to send out here. I could ask Darren. His wife has been having him do all sorts of projects lately, and with the slower time and no guests because of the wedding, he might have some time to work on them this weekend."

Sadie raised her head, knowing hope was clearly written on her face. "Would you? That would be amazing. I might need him to do a couple of other things as well, but I'll have to get some inspiration online."

"Why do you still seem down about the whole thing?" Evan's soothing voice caused her to lay her head back down and close her eyes. She could feel the swaying of her heart, working to break down all the barriers she'd erected around it to keep from getting hurt. As much as she felt confused about how he felt about her, she was sure she was falling, and at the moment, there was nothing she could do to stop herself.

Sighing, she sat up and tucked a piece of hair behind her ear, focusing on the table in front of them. "I had this vision of how perfect this wedding would be, how your sister would absolutely love it and it would wow Charleigh French. But at the moment, I'm doubting my abilities on both counts."

"You'll be fine. Just make sure to breathe and do what you can do. If you don't get the wedding for Charleigh, you'll get one somewhere else."

"Coming from Mr. Perfectionist who has a hard time if he doesn't get something right the first time." She turned her voice a bit lower, trying to make it sound like she was teasing him. But as she saw his face harden, his jaw tight, she knew she'd struck a nerve. Holding out her hands, she said, "I didn't mean it like that, Evan. It was a joke."

He stood, turning to her with a sad smile. "First I'm arrogant, and now I'm a perfectionist. Thanks for clueing me in to the reason I'm still single." He moved toward the door, taking long strides, and Sadie felt her heart rate pick up.

Standing, her head felt as if it was spinning like a top, but she pushed through it, hoping to get to him before he left. "Evan, please wait." She was grateful he stopped, allowing her to grab his arm as he still faced away from her. She wouldn't have been able to hold him there if she'd needed to with her depleted strength, but it calmed her frenzied mind.

He turned to look at her, that same mask of neutrality placed on the day she'd called him arrogant.

"I promise I meant it as a compliment. You're amazing, and you have so many talents. Sometimes I envy you for what looks like perfection on the outside."

His voice was soft and deep, with a measure of sadness, sending a chill up her spine. "I'm far from perfect, but thank you. I hope your headache gets better soon. Call me if you need something; otherwise, my staff is prepared to assist you."

He moved out the door, and Sadie wondered how she was going to make this up to him. The first worry that came to her mind was if he would still dance with her at the wedding.

So selfish. Why couldn't she worry more about his feelings than her own? As she mulled that over for a minute or two, she sank back onto the couch and closed her eyes. She'd learned to put her feelings first when she'd moved to college. She had no real experience in a relationship as she'd shut everyone out who'd even tried. But now, she wanted one more than ever, and she'd just effectively ostracized him. She was going to need something to fix all this.

Picking up her phone, she dialed Aubrey. She'd come to the rescue and help her see what she needed to do to win Evan over. It was a leap, but she'd need to figure it out now before she lost him forever.

$\mathcal{E}$van couldn't get his mind off Sadie's words for the next few days. Every move he made caused him to analyze whether or not it was a perfectionist tendency or just a smart business move. Aubrey had texted right as he'd gotten off the plane in California, telling him to stop by and see her.

It had felt like the days had passed like molasses, the hours taunting him as he kept thinking about work and Sadie. He hadn't remembered until she'd called him Mr. Perfectionist that Stacey had called him that once a few weeks before their wedding. Her tone had been more snide than Sadie's, but the feeling was the same.

He'd grown up pushing himself in sports and other aspects, getting frustrated when he didn't do it right on the first try. But he kept at it, knowing that with enough prac-tice, he could be just as good as the others around him. There were several awards boxed up in his parents' shed for his sports accomplishments and even a few academic ones.

Maybe that was why it had taken so long to get over the

broken wedding. It wasn't so much his ex-fiancée but rather the fact that it was something he couldn't really fix.

He pulled up to Aubrey and Sadie's apartment, parking along the curb. She must have seen him coming, because the door opened before he could knock.

"Hey, Ev. I'm glad you made it." Aubrey yawned, covering her mouth with her hand. "Sorry, I just woke up after an all-nighter. Come in." She waved him into the front room.

He'd only been there once or twice since the girls had moved into it right after graduation, but he was surprised by the simple touches on the walls and in the décor. It all reminded him of the swatches and samples Sadie had been working with at the hotel, and his chest ached at the thought of it. Why did he have to like her so much?

He took a seat on the comfortable couch, and it reminded him of the ones Isabelle had recommended he get for the hotel. Were women just really good at picking out comfortable furniture?

"What's up?" He leaned back, threading his fingers together and resting them behind his head.

"I just wanted to check in and see how things are going. Sadie said she was worried about you after the whole cake-tasting thing." Aubrey's eyebrows cinched together, looking at him with pity.

Of course Sadie would tell Aubrey all about that. But at least she was worried. That was a good sign, right?

"I'm fine. You don't need to worry about me. It was just the scene that threw me off. But I promise I won't have any more episodes during Taryn's wedding."

Aubrey slid onto the couch next to him, tucking her legs under her. "How are things with you and Sadie?" She gave him a small smile, and Evan was grateful she wasn't bouncing up and down on the couch.

"They're good, I guess. I think we're both under a lot of

stress right now." He glanced down at his fingers, trying to avoid his sister's gaze.

"Which means?"

Turning his head to look at her, he said, "She called me a perfectionist, and now I'm feeling self-conscious about it. Stacey said something similar at one point, and I guess I'm just nervous that if anything got serious, Sadie would leave me just like Stacey did." The words spilled out, and he finally realized it was petty to worry about. Like he'd been called a name as a kid and was whining about it. "Forget it."

"I don't think she meant it as a bad thing. I know she's liked you, and after seeing you two together at the festival, I know there's some chemistry there. I think you both just need to get it figured out. Just work together. You are the perfect balance for her, and she for you." She shrugged and smiled. "Just an outsider's opinion."

His next words came out in a whisper. "I like her a lot, but I don't think I can go through a broken heart again."

Aubrey moved closer, pulling him next to her. "You're good. Honestly, I don't know why you were with Stacey in the first place. I know she hurt you, but she would have manipulated you the rest of your life. So in a way, I wish I could thank her for leaving you alone so you can have the chance to find someone incredible, like Sadie."

Evan swallowed hard, the emotion making it difficult. He nodded. "I guess I won't know until I try."

"That's the Evan I know. The one who doesn't give up. Just don't think that's a bad thing." She gave him a look out of the corner of her eye, and Evan chuckled, grateful he'd come there.

Maybe he wasn't all broken.

CHAPTER 23

The day before the wedding arrived, and Sadie was more nervous than ever. The fact that Evan had been delayed coming back to Vegas had taken its toll on her, making her worried that she'd done irreparable damage to their relationship. She'd texted and called, trying to apologize over and over again without luck, until finally he said, "Don't worry about it. I'm good."

He'd arrived back early that morning, and although he seemed more like his normal self, there was something holding him back, as if he were afraid Sadie would hurt him again.

"How goes the decorating?" he asked, coming up behind her in the large event room. He glanced around, nodding, and Sadie wondered if that meant he approved.

"It's going. Would you mind helping me with this banner? I want it to hang between the pillars, and I've been trying to do it for some time by myself, with bad results."

He picked up the end she gave him and walked to where she requested. Holding it up, he waited for her to attach it on her end. He continued holding it until she walked up to him. The woodsy smell of him and the scruff on his face made Sadie want to lean up and kiss him, wanting a smile to take over his face as it had so many times over the past few weeks.

After staring at him a moment, she reached out to take his hand. The same electric pulse coursed through her hand and up to her shoulder, spreading from there to the rest of her body. "Please tell me you're not still mad at me." She stared into his hazel eyes, wanting to get lost in them and put all that had happened between them in the past.

The side of his mouth turned up, and he shook his head. "No, I'm not mad about that. I just didn't realize how tired I am. I feel like I've been working like crazy over the past few weeks. I won't know the results of the five-diamond award until the beginning of next year."

Sadie bit her tongue, knowing another comment about perfection wouldn't go over well with him. "Well, we're less than twenty-four hours from the start of the wedding, and then you can get back to managing your hotel like normal. I'll be out of your hair before you know it."

His face softened, and she was surprised when he gathered her into his arms. He held her there for several seconds, and something poured between them, a sense of calm that she hadn't felt since he'd held her on the swing in his parents' backyard.

He pulled back enough that Sadie could see the emotions playing across his face. "I'm in no rush for you to leave, but I do need to go get some work done before everything goes crazy tomorrow. How have the events gone?"

Sadie nodded. "Really well. You're not going shooting with the guys? I think they leave in an hour."

Glancing down at his watch, realization dawned, and he said, "I'd better go. Otherwise, they'll never let me live it down." He leaned forward, pressing a kiss to her forehead, and gave her a smile.

Sadie watched him go, feeling like she'd just thrown herself off the cliff and was freefalling. To what end, she still didn't know. This was why she'd guarded her heart for all those years, because the thought of not knowing the outcome scared her. Her life had been just fine without dredging up an old crush on her best friend's brother, and she hoped she'd survive when this was all done.

Aubrey appeared in the doorway. "Are you ready, gal? We've got appointments for manis and pedis downstairs, and you're coming with."

"But I have all this I have to get done."

Taking a step back, Aubrey waved some people in. "I asked Evan's staff to help out. Now, tell them where you want everything and come relax with the girls. It will help take your mind off of everything. They'll get the bulk of it all done, and then we can make minor changes and adjustments later tonight."

Sadie bit her lip, not sure she wanted to chance that. What if they put things up in the wrong places? She'd worked on her own for so long, only having a handful of people to help her decorate. But this might be a nice change. And she could definitely use a day at the spa to feel better.

After fifteen minutes of in-depth instructions about where everything would go, Sadie gave the room one last look before Aubrey pulled her away and to the elevator, punching the down arrow.

"What's wrong?" she asked Sadie.

"It will just be nice for the wedding to be over. There has been so much pressure leading up to it that I hope I do it justice."

"You're worrying about what Charleigh will think of it, aren't you?"

"A little."

Aubrey turned, trying to look into her eyes. "Is this about Evan?"

Moving her lips to the side, Sadie finally raised her eyes to look at her best friend. "Maybe."

A wide smile spread across her face. "The last you told me, you had a crush on him again, but that was it." She wiggled her eyebrows, making Sadie laugh.

"I know I said I would never have a relationship—"

"Which I've always told you was bologna," Aubrey said, cutting her off.

Sadie rolled her eyes. "Well, I really like him, like more-than-just-a-crush like him."

The elevator doors finally opened, and they stepped inside, Aubrey pressing the button for the shops on the floor below. She clapped her hands together and did a little dance, looking like she'd just opened up the best Christmas present ever.

"Why do you seem sad about it?" she asked.

"Because I keep getting mixed signals from him. And I don't think he's forgiven me for the perfectionist and arrogant comments. Why can't I just keep my mouth shut?"

Aubrey wrapped an arm around Sadie's shoulders and pulled her in. "But maybe that's what will be the trump card for you. He's always had trouble finding girls who like him for his personality instead of looks, and now money. You're the one calling him out on how he can better himself, and I think, in the long run, it will help sway the vote in your favor."

"When you say it like that, it makes me sound like I'm already perfect, when we know I'm far from that." Blowing out a breath, Sadie was glad to see the elevator open and dozens of people milling about, in and out of the underground shops. "Where is your mom and everyone else?"

"I told them we'd meet them at the spa. We've got quite the day ahead, and I think we should do a few extra things for you." Aubrey grinned, the look mischievous.

Holding up her hands, Sadie shook her head. "No, I'm the wedding planner. I'm not a bridesmaid or anyone who is supposed to be visible. I wear black and have my hair in a ponytail the entire time, with a headset glued to my mouth so I can communicate with everyone I need to. As much as I'd love to dress up, that's not part of the job description."

Aubrey smiled. "We'll take care of all that. If it will help you have the best night ever and break through the wall of rules you've made for yourself over the past ten years, I'll do it. I don't have a guy to worry about, and I'm sorry, but Travis's younger brother is only sixteen, so no temptation there. The rest is family. You're the one with the opportunity of a lifetime."

Rolling her eyes again, Sadie said, "Please. I'm sure your brother just sees me as your best friend, the nerdy girl who always had a crush on him in high school." But as she said those words, she could still feel his lips against her forehead and the tender way he'd kissed her lips back at the ranch.

"Well, you're not nerdy anymore. And I think he has a thing for you too."

But would they be able to make it work? A guy who had fears about weddings and a girl who wasn't sure she would be good at a long-term relationship after what her own parents had been through. They'd be quite the pair.

As they walked into the spa, Taryn, Dolores, Aubrey's grandmother, and a handful of other relatives who were lined up in the chairs for pedicures cheered as they saw them enter. Aubrey led Sadie over to the row of ladies waiting to do manicures.

"Pick a fun color, and then we'll find you a dress to match."

As silly as it sounded, Sadie was filled with more hope than she'd had in quite some time.

CHAPTER 24

"Why are you looking all put out? I thought shooting with the guys was your idea?" Aiden bumped Evan with his elbow and raised his eyebrow with a question on his face.

"Long day. Long month, I should say. How are things with you?"

Aiden grinned and loaded his rifle, waiting for his turn in the line of guys shooting at clay pigeons on the outskirts of Vegas. "Going well. We just made it through another major update of Quickstagram, and am I glad to have that one in the books. Hopefully, it will improve the use and speed of it."

Evan nodded, thinking that over. He never could have come up with something like that, needing tangible things to work with rather than code. But Aiden had always been good at that, contrary to what everyone who'd ever met them thought. Even though they were identical twins, they still had a lot of differences in likes and dislikes.

"How are things with Sadie?"

Evan turned his head and frowned at his brother. "What do you mean?"

"Aubrey said you two were getting kind of close. I just thought I'd ask to see if she's won over your guarded heart."

Groaning, Evan should have suspected that his triplet sister would say something about the spark of interest he had in Sadie. Okay, it was more like a roaring fire at this point, and every attempt at squelching the thoughts and feelings was failing. The idea of liking someone that much while working to pick out items for a wedding, let alone prepare for one, made his insides disagree with his brain.

If only he'd known then what he knew now, he could have avoided proposing to Stacey and wouldn't have gone through all the pain, thinking he'd lost out on his dreams. To not feel like he was enough for Stacey only drove him to push harder. What Sadie called the perfectionist in him had been working in rampant mode over the last five years.

"Well, she thinks I'm an arrogant perfectionist, so that's about as well as it's going." His tone was harsher than he'd meant it to sound. He'd forgiven her for the comments, so why was he still irritated? Because he hadn't done much to change just yet?

Aiden grinned. "Sounds like she's a keeper, then. You've always complained about girls liking you for alternate motives. She knows just about everything there is to know about you and still has interest."

Evan mulled that over, wondering if his brother was right. She was blunt, and he wasn't used to that at all, not since Coach Montgomery, anyway. He'd learned so much and had been able to change from the feedback Coach had given him. Maybe a little criticism from Sadie wasn't a bad thing.

As he thought about the retreat with the IBC guys, he wished it were sooner, feeling exhaustion wash over him. He'd been working hard since that day five years ago, and he hadn't really stopped more than a day or two. He wanted more of what he'd had while visiting the ranch a few weeks before, a slower pace. Could he have that while still managing a successful hotel business?

It was something he'd need to find out. But if he could slow down, and Sadie did return his feelings, would he even know how to work that out? She'd be traveling all the time for weddings. Would he go with her, or would that be too much strain?

Too many questions for a simple shooting outing with the guys.

"I don't know, bro," he finally said. "I guess we'll see how things turn out."

Aiden moved into position to shoot, nailing each of the clay pigeons as they were thrown. Evan was up next, and for the first time in his life, he missed each and every target.

Every eye was on him, most with their mouths agape at the fact that he'd missed so many. He usually won every contest, had been the best at everything or had worked at it until he was. But it seemed as though ever since Sadie had called all that into question, he couldn't function the same. Was his life falling apart because of it?

"That's a first," Darren said, slapping Evan on the back. "Welcome back to earth with the rest of us mortals, Ev." He grinned.

A thought rang through. Evan had always delighted in being the best at everything he tried, but his older brother stood in front of him now, imperfect at best but a man with a loving wife and a growing family. Would it go against every-thing inside him to be okay with average?

Not that Sadie was average, but would she be okay with seeing his faults and imperfections, the slight insecurities that plagued him daily? He'd just have to figure that out. For the first time, a glimmer of hope welled up in his chest.

* * *

Aubrey held up a long silver dress in front of Sadie. "It's your size. Try it on." Glancing at the tag, Sadie's eyes grew wide.

"There's no way I can afford that, even with the pay I get from wedding planning. I would throw up just knowing how much it cost." Sadie took a step back, trying to keep herself from touching the fabric. The dress was beautiful, and she could picture herself in it, but not for tens of thousands of dollars.

Whipping out a card, Aubrey grinned. "Let's not worry about price right now."

Frowning, Sadie said, "Aubrey, there's no way you can pay that much for a dress either."

"But it's not my card. It's Evan's."

"Why do you have his card?" Sadie folded her arms and averted her eyes from the dress, the temptation to try it on pulling at her with each second that ticked past.

Wiggling her eyebrows, Aubrey said, "Because he told me to put all the expenses from today on it."

"That doesn't mean he okayed a fifteen-thousand-dollar dress." Sadie moved away, glancing at the other dresses in the couture store. One caught her eye, a dark blue satin that looked like it would hit around her knees. She could wear that while getting everything ready before the wedding and still look more dressed up than usual.

Pulling it off the rack, she looked it over, liking the ruffles along the front.

"That is a cute one. But are you sure you don't want the silver one?"

Shaking her head, Sadie said, "I'm not buying a dress on your brother's card, no matter how much or how little it costs."

"Why not?"

"Because I can buy my own. I think I'll try this one on." She took the dress to the dressing room and pulled it on, wishing it wasn't so tight around her curves.

"I want to see it before you take it off." Aubrey's voice was more sing-song than anything.

Sadie sighed, walking out of the room. With a twirl, she pretended to strike a pose, imitating a model at the end of the runway.

Aubrey's finger was over her mouth and tapping away. "I like it, but I don't love it."

"Well, find something I can afford," Sadie said, pointing her finger and raising an eyebrow. Her best friend grinned and turned around, moving to look through some more dresses.

Sadie changed back into her clothes, deciding she'd have to look as well or they'd either be there all day, or Aubrey would convince her to buy something way out of her budget.

An hour and fifteen dresses later, Sadie walked out of the high-end store with an emerald-green dress that Aubrey was convinced matched Sadie's eyes.

"Okay, now for shoes."

Sadie loved to shop as much as the next girl, but with as picky as Aubrey was being about everything, she was more worn out than she cared to admit, and she still had a long night ahead.

"How about you pick something for me? You know my size. Nothing sky-high, though. I still need to be able to walk."

Aubrey winked at her. "Okay, but no flats. We've got to show off those legs of yours."

At her comment, Sadie pictured Evan looking at her legs, and she was suddenly self-conscious. Maybe she needed a longer dress because now she wasn't going to survive without worrying about him staring at her throughout the entire wedding.

"Just make sure they're sensible. I've got to get back upstairs to make sure everything is ready for the rehearsal dinner."

Waving Aubrey off, Sadie made her way back up to the event room. The staff had done a great job with most of the decorations, transforming the nice big room into the vision in her head. White fabric had been draped from the center and then out at several points, along with white twinkle lights, and she could picture what it would look like with the lights off.

Chairs were set up on one half of the room and tables on the other, making the best use of the space to transform from a ceremony to the reception. That was one of the requests Taryn made that Sadie had been all for, having the ceremony and the reception back-to-back. While it was a little stressful to get everything set up at first, it made it nice so that they didn't have to wait for hours and the two could escape to their honeymoon sooner.

In the corner sat several rustic wood planters, and when she saw Darren the next day, she would have to kiss him for helping her out on such short notice. He'd also put together several square plank pieces which she would use around the food displays to add that rustic touch.

Taking the planters, she started arranging them on the tables, figuring they would work for the rehearsal dinner which started in less than two hours. It was easier to get as much decorated in the wee hours of the morning as she could so she didn't have to worry about accidentally sleeping in or not having the time to fix any problems that might arise.

With the pint-sized mason jars settled into each of the planters, she worked to tie white and pink burlap pieces around the base, tying into the theme of the wedding and adding a pop of color to the table.

"If I didn't know any better, I'd say you are a workaholic." Evan's smooth, deep voice caused her to jump a bit before turning around and smiling at him.

"That could be true, except I spent the day being pampered with your family." Something about her words made him smile, and he came and sat in one of the white folding chairs next to her.

"I just missed every shot I took with my family. Which is a first." His gaze locked onto hers, and she tried to hide a shudder as a chill spread throughout her.

Turning to focus on the burlap, she smiled. "From what I can remember, you didn't miss often." She wasn't sure what she was trying to imply, only leaving the statement alone and focusing to get the look of the bow just right.

Evan drummed his fingers along the table, causing Sadie to glance up. "What are your plans for tonight?" he asked, looking relaxed against the seat.

Sadie couldn't help but contain a laugh as she gestured toward the room. "Look around you. I've got a rehearsal dinner in ninety minutes, a wedding happening in less than twenty-four hours, and a reception after. I could use some help, though." She grinned at him, watching his expression range from disgust to uncertainty.

"Are you all right? You don't have to if it's too much for you," she said, realizing he might not be up for dealing with more wedding-related jobs that dredged up old memories. She'd concluded that this was the bulk of why he was acting weird lately, that the idea of planning and even participating in a wedding was throwing him off. At least, she hoped that was true.

"Yeah, I'll be fine. What can I do?" He frowned as he

looked at the table, and Sadie held in a laugh so he wouldn't run off.

"Why don't you get the planters from the wall over there and bring them here?"

He nodded and retrieved them, bringing several in one trip. As he placed them on the table, she saw his strong hands as they let go of the handles and remembered his hand holding hers. Why had everything she could remember happened in Aspen Hollow?

He grimaced. "Do you need me to help you tie bows?"

Sadie laughed, tilting her head back and glancing at the ceiling. "No. I won't torture you completely. But I wouldn't mind some company while I tie them. How was California?"

He started talking, and Sadie was glad he was slipping back into the Evan she'd started to fall in love with several weeks ago. Her crush on him had always been just that, but getting to know him more over the past few weeks, she'd come to see there was a lot more underneath the surface. She just hoped he'd be able to make it through this wedding, or at least let her help him through it.

CHAPTER 25

*E*van shook his head as he walked down to the parking garage. He was proud of himself for sticking around to help Sadie, even though it was more talking than actual helping. Seeing all of the work that went into the wedding and seeing Sadie at the center of it did something to his brain, and he hoped he'd made some progress in getting over his past trauma of being dumped on his wedding day.

He'd gone back to his room and arrived "late" for the rehearsal dinner, hoping that they'd have the actual rehearsal part of it done by the time he arrived. But in true Taryn fashion, they'd only just begun when he came down. Sadie had been within earshot, and the thought of saying "corn dogs" crossed his mind, but he was determined to make it through this part tonight and deal with the rest in the morning.

He'd thought about requesting George to take him for a drive, but he needed the feel of control and the ability to speed to get all the anxiety out of his system.

At least he wasn't the best man and wouldn't have to be

front and center all the time like he'd been at his own failed wedding.

What he needed was a way to break through the fog and the disappointment. How could he resolve the one thing that had been niggling at him for the last five years, especially when he hadn't connected with anyone but a girl who'd committed to never marry?

He'd only been back in Vegas for a few hours, and he already wished he could return to one of the hotels he owned in California. It had been easier to put his mind to work rather than consistently dredging up the old memories of the wedding again. It was as though he was beaten down with each memory, feeling like he wasn't good enough, that he didn't measure up. With the many things he'd accomplished over the years, his failure seemed to be shining through, no matter how much he tried to cover it up in his mind.

No amount of training, no award, could give him what he now wanted more than ever: a wife and family. But would he end up in the same position if he moved further with Sadie? He didn't want to think about going through heartbreak again.

Evan raced down a back road in the dark of night, feeling the speed pull something free inside him. It was small, but it was enough relief to allow the rest of him to relax a bit.

As he thought more about Jackson, Tristan, and Roman, he realized they had all conquered their pasts, each finding a woman who adored them, or kept them in line, or both. Evan grinned as he thought about it, especially Jackson's relationship with Hailey, Coach Montgomery's daughter. But the sisters, Juliette and Isabelle, weren't mild either, each of them having a fiery personality to help Tristan and Roman.

His thoughts turned to Sadie, and he wondered if she could really be that for him. Could she handle moving from hotel to hotel as each project moved forward? She already did that somewhat for weddings, but the more Evan thought about it, the more he realized how much he wanted something more simple, more settled. He would probably always have to travel, but if he could make it less and train the right people to take over his hotels, he just might find that peace he needed, maybe even with the one he needed.

Blue and red lights flashed behind him, and Evan tapped the steering wheel with his hand. He'd been so focused on what was going on in his mind that he hadn't been looking for cops. Pulling over, he took out his wallet and insurance information, ready to hand it to the man as he walked up.

"Driver's license and registration." The cop bent down so he could see through the window, a flashlight blinding Evan at one point.

Evan handed the papers to the man and waited.

After several seconds of staring at the information, the man asked, "Where are you heading, and do you know how fast you were going?"

"I was just out for a drive to get some air. I wasn't looking at the speedometer." Evan had never been good at lying, especially under pressure like this, so it was best to just admit the truth.

"Well, you certainly got a lot of air, then, because you were going at least twenty miles over the speed limit. And that was after you put on the brakes."

"I'm sorry, sir. My sister is getting married tomorrow, and I'm not good with weddings."

The man looked into his eyes, making Evan feel self-conscious. After several awkward seconds, he said, "Give me a few minutes to process this information."

Evan nodded and leaned his head on the headrest. This was just what he needed tonight.

After a few minutes, the cop came back. "I've reduced the speeding to nine over, so you won't be reported to your insurance company. Call it an early wedding gift for your sister that you're not in jail right now."

A measure of relief passed through Evan, and he gave the man a tight smile. "I will. Thank you, sir."

Rolling the window back up, Evan turned the car around and drove at a leisurely pace back to the hotel. He didn't need to get hit with another ticket tonight, and at the rate his luck was falling, he'd end up behind bars. His mother wouldn't be too happy about that, and neither would his sisters. But the one person he didn't feel like disappointing right now was Sadie.

CHAPTER 26

By the time she'd finished cleaning up after the dinner and setting up the rest of the event hall, Sadie had only slept about three hours the night before. Now, at seven in the morning, she had done all she could to cover the signs of tiredness that covered her face and went back to work.

The flowers were being delivered in the next hour, and with the confirmation of the food from Tom, most everything was ready, at least she hoped.

How are you doing?

Her fingers paused over the keyboard on her phone, trying to figure out what else to send to Evan. He'd said something about needing some air the night before, and as much as she'd have loved to go with him, he looked like he just needed out of the hotel.

She pushed send and tucked her phone into her back pocket, ready to arrange flowers.

A few hours later, at noon, Sadie went to check on the bridal party in one of the larger suites near the one Sadie was staying in. Walking in, it seemed like a mass of women bustling about, curlers in hair and most of them not quite ready to go yet.

She looked around and spotted Aubrey over next to Taryn, curling her sister's hair. Sadie's best friend had always been good with hair, and had she not had an interest in nursing, she probably would have become a cosmetologist.

"Sadie, I'm so glad you're up here. How are things?" Taryn smiled, but the look seemed off, not brightening her entire face like Sadie was used to. Nerves. Even someone as confident and prepared for life as Taryn was a little nervous on her wedding day.

Holding up her hand, Sadie gave the signal for okay. "Everything is set up for the ceremony and reception. We have all the flowers delivered, and I just finished arranging them in the different areas around the hall. The food will be here shortly, and I just wanted to check on all of you before I head over to make sure the guys are ready."

Sadie heard something tear behind her and turned to see the panicked look on the face of one of the two other bridesmaids. Walking over to her, Sadie smiled.

"Just take it off for a second. I'll get it fixed in a couple of minutes, and you'll be good to go." Pulling her shirt up a few inches, Sadie pulled a needle and thread out of a small fanny pack she kept hidden during weddings for this purpose. She'd loved watching *The Wedding Planner* as a girl, and it was that innovative idea that had saved her more times than she could even count during the weddings she'd planned.

After quickly stitching the seam over the shoulder, Sadie handed it back to the girl, helping her pull it up so the stitches wouldn't be under any force to pull them apart.

When that was done, she moved back to the Pearson clan. "Okay, how are things over here?"

"We are doing well, Sadie, dear. Why don't you sit down

so we can get you ready as well?" Dolores Pearson said with a grin.

Holding up a hand, Sadie backed a step or two away. "I'd love to, but right now I need to make sure there is a groom and groomsmen waiting, or at least getting ready."

"What do you mean, 'make sure there's a groom'? Travis is here, right?" Taryn's eyes flashed, and she looked toward the door as if she could see right through it.

Realizing her mistake, Sadie shook her head. "I'm sorry. I...I'm sure he's there. I just meant I need to go check on them. You know how guys can be a little mischievous." The panic wasn't leaving Taryn's face, and Sadie decided she'd better keep her mouth shut and leave before she left the girl in tears.

Not that she would be planning her own wedding anytime soon, but for some reason, all the little details were sticking out to her, making her take note of it all. She'd been a part of many weddings with her business, but something was different this time. She wished she could just chalk it up to the wedding being for a family friend, but a sliver of hope burned in her chest as she wished it was the idea that she could get married someday, and maybe even to Evan.

But after his weird behavior the last two days, she'd be surprised if he'd ever propose again. Weddings were something she found fun and exciting for other people, but she could understand why he was so hesitant about most of it.

Escaping down the hall to the other end, she knocked on the door of the suite that was supposed to hold all the men connected to the wedding: Travis, his best man, Aiden, Evan, Darren, their father, and a few uncles who were part of the wedding.

The door opened, and Sadie's heart skipped a beat for a moment, until she realized it was Aiden, the small scar near his eye giving it away.

"Sadie. It's good to see you today. Are you here to check up on us?" Aiden gave her a half-grin and moved to the side so she could pass.

"Maybe. How is everything here? Do we have all the neckties? Cummerbunds? Rings?" She looked around at each of the men sitting around the room watching some sports reel and shook her head. The women were all stressed about getting ready and looking their best while the guys weren't even in their suits yet.

"I think we're good so far, Sadie." Travis broke his gaze away from the television long enough to say that and smile at her, his attention swaying seconds after.

Evan stood from the couch and made his way over, his smile wider than it had been in days. Maybe he was finally feeling better. She could only hope.

"Hey, how are you?" he asked after Aiden had moved to sit next to their father on the bed. His tone was casual, as if they were just hanging out, but his face said something different, something she couldn't read yet. She worked to focus on his face, as the white shirt and the black tuxedo pants made her insides buzz.

She smiled at him. "Tired, but good. Just trying to make sure everything goes off without a hitch. How are you? Did you get my text earlier?"

"Yeah, I'm sorry I didn't respond yet. I'm good. I went for a drive last night and ended up with a speeding ticket. But at least I feel a little more myself." Evan put a hand in his pocket and studied her face. She was tempted to reach up and kiss him, but she didn't want to do it in front of all the guys, even though their eyes were glued to the TV.

"I can understand that. Do you want me to tie that?" She pointed to the bow tie slung around his neck and stepped closer. Her hands moved without concentration as she'd done this a few times. She could feel his eyes on her face, and her breathing picked up speed as she took in the smell of his cologne. She used both hands to smooth the bow tie and let them trail down a bit before she looked up at him.

There was something unreadable in his expression, but one corner of his mouth turned up, and Sadie couldn't help but smile.

"Thanks for that. I've never been good at tying bow ties."

She opened her mouth, debating whether she should say anything in response. "Just another reason we'd make a great team." Her eyes widened, and she bit her upper lip, wondering where that comment had come from. Stumbling a few steps back, she spoke again, her voice much louder than it should have been, causing all the guys to turn in her direction.

"Okay, well, call me if there is an emergency here. We've now got..." Sadie looked at her watch, "...about forty-five minutes until the ceremony starts, so make sure this highlight reel doesn't keep you from getting ready."

Evan nodded, opening the door for her. "Will do." He placed a hand on Sadie's arm, feeling like a lit fire, and she stopped when his voice dropped to a lower octave. "You're still planning on dancing with me tonight, right?"

Sadie looked up at him through her lashes with a shy smile. "I wouldn't miss it."

The look on his face made her insides feel as if they were going to explode with excitement, and she hurried out into the hall, not wanting to ruin the moment they'd just had. Why was she so worried about what he wanted? She really just needed to focus on getting through this day and hopefully getting the contract with Charleigh French.

CHAPTER 27

*E*van stood in line at the front of the event hall, sticking a finger in between his collar and his neck. He gave it a good tug and was able to breathe for a minute or two before it seemed like the fabric would cut off his oxygen altogether.

He stood with Darren in front of him, and Aiden behind, which gave him the comfort that if he fainted, he'd be supported, and if he tried to flee, his brothers would keep him from going too far. The doors opened, and in walked several of the guests, taking their seats somewhere in the back.

Focusing on breathing in through his nose and out through his mouth, Evan focused on the banner hanging between the columns across from him. It reminded him of Sadie, of how she took such great care in every detail. He looked around for her, wondering if she would be able to sit in the hall for the wedding or if she was coordinating something in the background.

The doors opened and music played, but no one came through for several seconds, triggering the panic to take over in his chest. His sister wouldn't do the same thing as Stacey, would she?

Darren's little girl, Stephanie, walked through the doors, her steps quick for a four-year-old flower girl. Behind her were the two bridesmaids, friends of Taryn's from college. Evan's breathing evened out a bit more as the women came down the aisle, lining up on the other side. When he finally saw Aubrey walk in, Evan grinned as she made a face at him. She always knew how to help him relax.

The song changed to "Wedding March," and the crowd of people all stood, turning to look toward the bride. Their father was escorting Taryn down the aisle, and the thing Evan noticed most was the wide grin across her face. She looked so happy, like she couldn't believe this was happening to her.

Evan could only see Travis's profile, but a tear ran down the guy's cheek. Was this supposed to be what weddings were like? Because in all of his experiences with them, he still wasn't sure what the protocol was for one.

The vows began, and he did his best to focus, hoping his nervous system wouldn't give out on him right then. Pulling out his phone, he hid it behind Darren's back. He opened a message to Sadie and typed, *Corn dogs.*

He slid the device back into his pocket and looked around the room, hoping to see her somewhere, anywhere. Her calming influence was what he needed most right then.

A minute or two later, he felt something touch his hand, and he turned, looking at the backdrop. A hand had taken his, and through the lattice, he saw Sadie, understanding written on her face. Her hair was curled, and she had a light touch of makeup on her face. Her beauty took away his fears for a few seconds, and he felt the tension in his shoulders relax.

In a faint whisper that couldn't be heard over the

pastor's voice, she said, "I'm here. You can do this." She held his hand for a few more minutes and then signaled that she had to take care of something in the kitchen. The loss of her hand in his felt worse than anything he'd ever gone through after Stacey left, and he knew his heart belonged to Sadie.

Once the bride and groom had said the "I do's," Evan breathed a sigh of relief and was even more grateful when they took off down the aisle and out of the hall. Groups of people joined together, chatting and catching up.

Evan moved about the room, trying to see if Sadie was around somewhere. He looked in several places, even knocking on her suite. Had she left?

With a bitter taste on his tongue, he walked back to the elevator and punched in the button for the penthouse. He needed a moment before he could go back and face everyone at the reception.

* * *

It seemed like all Sadie had done was clean up mess after mess. She should have known that the calm always came before the storm, especially when it came to weddings. After she'd checked on the guys, she'd gone back to the bridal suite and let Aubrey curl her hair and put on a little bit of makeup.

"I have to leave in thirty minutes, even if you've only done one side of my hair," she threatened her friend.

Aubrey chuckled but worked fast, curling the hair and then braiding the top half of it. When she was done, Sadie grinned, noticing the auburn tint of her hair pulled out by small green gems Aubrey had placed in the waves.

She felt beautiful and ecstatic, wondering what Evan's reaction would be. But all that faded from her mind as she arrived in the kitchen to find that the top layer of the cake had fallen to the ground, and several of the flowers were sliding down the side of the cake.

"Tom, what happened?" She tried to keep her voice as calm as possible, knowing that making her caterer agitated before the event even started would make for a rough day all around.

"I'm so sorry, Miss Sadie. I'm doing what I can to fix it." The man kept pulling things out of his coat and sticking them into the cake. She just hoped Taryn wouldn't take a bite and end up chewing on a toothpick.

Pulling an apron from one of the hooks near the wall, Sadie wrapped it around herself, moving into survival mode.

"Okay, what can I do?"

Tom directed her to one of the guys in the kitchen. She blended and mixed the cream frosting for the top layer, and the guy was able to create the top layer and bake it, all within the time they had before the ceremony started, which was a miracle of itself.

She heard the ding of a text message, and once she saw Evan's S.O.S., she ran out and did the best she could to comfort him. She'd been flattered that he would reach out to her, especially when surrounded by family. And the way he'd looked at her through the lattice took her breath away. Her feelings for him were skyrocketing, and as much as she didn't want to, she had to motion that she had to return to the kitchen, hoping to finalize the design of the cake.

With Aubrey's help, Sadie was able to get out of the kitchen a few minutes after the bride and groom had disappeared. She took a look in the mirror, trying not to grimace at the cake on her apron. Thank goodness it wasn't on her dress.

Many of the guests had already filtered over to the reception side of the event hall, and Sadie could hear Aubrey say Taryn wasn't quite ready yet.

Frowning, Sadie wondered what could have taken them so long. The bride had been wearing her dress only moments before. Wouldn't a simple makeup check be all that she needed?

Sadie clued in the catering people and made sure everything was set for whenever the bride and groom made their entrance again.

"Are you Sadie Gibson?" a voice called over her shoulder.

Turning, Sadie found herself staring into the eyes of Charleigh French. The girl looked younger in person, as well as shorter than she'd pictured.

"Miss French, how nice to see you. I'm glad you were able to make it out to the wedding today." Sadie reached her hand forward, and Charleigh shook it.

"We did. My fiancé is over there talking with some of the other guests, but it looks like you were able to pull this off rather quickly. One of the guests was saying in only six weeks?"

From her tone of voice, Sadie couldn't tell if that was a compliment or a cut. Nodding, she said, "Yes, the bride came to me around the beginning of October, and I've been here working on getting all the plans together for the last few weeks."

Charleigh looked around. "Wow! That's incredible. I always thought I wanted the modern, classic style, but all the little touches here make me reconsider. It's so well-done."

Sadie felt like her insides would burst with excitement and did her best to smile, nodding and saying, "Thank you. I really appreciate that."

"From all that we've researched about you and your prior weddings, I would love for you to plan our wedding in June. Would you be up for that?"

"I would love it. I'll make sure to plug it into my calendar, and we can get started planning it right after the new year. I have a client getting married two days before Christmas, and then I'm available to get to work on your wedding."

"Thank you so much, Sadie. I really appreciate it, and I can't wait to see what you come up with for us." She squeezed Sadie's forearm and then moved in the direction of her fiancé.

Everything inside Sadie wanted to scream with excitement. She hadn't believed she had a shot at getting the celebrity wedding, but with the simple touches and being flexible for Taryn, it had paid off.

Aubrey sauntered over wearing a pale pink dress, her hair half-up and curled at the ends. "Looks like you got some good news. Was that Charleigh French?"

Sadie nodded. "She said she wants me to do it! Can you believe that?" The two girls came together dancing and squealing softly.

Aubrey wrapped her arms around Sadie and gave her a hug. "I'm so excited for you, girl. Your career is taking off, and I love it. Now all you need is a supportive man by your side, and you'll be good."

At her words, Sadie turned, scanning the room for an attractive male. But after sweeping the room twice, she realized he wasn't there. With the rest of the family now on one side of the room, all fussing around the bride who'd just opened the gift Sadie and Dolores had worked hard to make, a personalized quilt with pictures and messages from each family member, she was sure Evan would be there. She again mistook Aiden for Evan before feeling the same disappointment as she'd had at the door earlier that day.

"Where's Evan?" she finally asked Aubrey.

Aubrey turned to look around the room, her eyes moving quickly but not locking on to anything. "I don't see him. You get things started here, and I'll go look for him. I wouldn't want him to miss out on dancing with you in that dress."

Sadie felt her cheeks turn warm, and she looked down at the dress. The color made her feel confident, and it was comfortable enough to work in, which was a feat considering how many times she'd had to bend down and reach for things.

Dinner began, and she heard compliment after compliment about the food. When the praise came from the Pearson family, though, she knew it was genuine. The toasts began, and Sadie laughed during the best man's speech and then teared up as Aubrey spoke about her only sister and how excited she was for this new adventure for the two of them.

Once the speeches were over, she walked up to Aubrey and whispered, "Any sign of him?"

Aubrey's face turned solemn, and she nodded her head. "I searched his office, and Brent let me into the penthouse. He was asleep on the bed."

Glancing around the room, Sadie pulled off her headphone and handed it to Aubrey. "I'll go check on him. He was having a tough time last night and during the ceremony." She explained the buttons in a quick sentence and said, "Make sure the dessert bar is stocked and that the tables get moved for the first dance. It should be ready for about thirty minutes from now."

Eyes wide, Aubrey looked as though she hadn't considered Evan's troubles. "I didn't even think about how today would affect him. It feels like so long ago that he was going to get married that I almost forgot about it. Maybe he just needs some time."

Sadie wouldn't be able to be gone for long, but she wanted to make sure Evan was okay.

As she waited for the elevator, the doors opened, revealing a worn Evan rubbing the back of his neck.

"Are you all right?" Sadie asked, waiting for him to step

out of the elevator. Once he did, she threw her arms around him, hoping the hug would infuse him with some comfort.

He gave her a small smile. "I'm better now. I could get used to seeing your face every day." He paused a moment, as he glanced at the dress and back to her face. "You look stunning."

Sadie blushed and led him in the direction of the event room. "I was a little worried you weren't going to show for our dance."

He shook his head. "I came to find you after the ceremony, but you were nowhere. I just needed a few minutes to relax before I had to endure more. Everything in small doses."

She took his hand and squeezed it, hoping he could understand that she was there for him, no matter what happened. "I need to get back to check on things. I left Aubrey in charge, and I'm a little worried about what might happen while she has that kind of power."

Evan laughed, the sound coming from deep down. "I get that. If you work now, you'll be able to dance with me." He winked at her, and she rose onto tiptoes, brushing her lips across his quickly. She smiled and turned, moving in the direction of the girl in the pink dress.

It was soon time for the first dance on the dance floor and Sadie watched with pride as Taryn danced with Travis, the two of them grinning at each other like children, stealing a kiss here and there as they moved to the music. Evan sat at the table his family was at, pushing the food around on his plate. She figured Dolores had saved food for him, but it was probably cold by that point.

Sadie directed a few guests to the restrooms, and when she turned back, Taryn was dancing with her father, the two of them swaying to an old tune, and something caught in Sadie's chest. This was one of the reasons she'd put off having a real relationship. Because who would she have to give her away? Her father hadn't spoken to her in years, and her mother would still be on parole for some crime. There was nothing she could do to recreate a father figure, unless she asked Carl Pearson directly.

Turning away, Sadie saw one of the people on her team and said, "I have to run to get something. Will you make sure everything is in order until I get back?"

The young woman nodded, and Sadie left the room just as tears broke through the dam she'd set in place so long ago. Just another strike against her. Evan had the perfect family, and hers was practically nonexistent.

She thought about going back in and finding Evan for a dance. Dancing with him had been something she'd looked forward to for longer than she wanted to admit, but now that he'd come back to the reception, she wondered how she could have dreamed a future could happen between them. He looked like he was barely surviving this wedding. This was her business, her livelihood. Would he be able to handle an afterwork chat everyday about weddings?

She thought about the rest of the Pearson family. The oldest brother, Darren, loved his wife, who fit into the family like she'd lived with them since the day she was born. And thinking of Travis and his family, he was basically a shoo-in for a perfect in-law.

Sadie had been grateful on so many occasions that Dolores and Carl had taken her in and helped her deal with her dysfunctional family when she was younger, but would that care transfer when it came to being with their son now?

Heading to freshen up in her suite, she took more time than usual, hoping that most of the people would be gone by the time she got down there to organize the cleanup. She was far from wanting to talk to people and just needed to get through the night.

A call came in, and Sadie recognized the number as being for the bride of the wedding set two days before Christmas. "Hi, Brooke. How are you?"

A sniffle came through the phone. "Our venue was double-booked. Since the other couple reserved it two months before we did, we're out. What are we going to do?"

The problem-solving wedding planner in Sadie moved into action, putting her worries aside. "I'm just finishing up a wedding tonight. I'll be on the first flight out tomorrow morning, and we'll figure it out. Don't you worry, girl."

Maybe some time away would be good. She needed the beach, the fresh air and the crash of the waves on the sand. That would hopefully put her life into perspective.

CHAPTER 28

When Evan woke up, it was nearly noon the next day. He found himself curled up on the couch in his penthouse, still dressed in his wedding attire. It took a moment for his brain to register what had happened the night before. Sadie had come looking for him, had said she was excited to dance with him at the reception, but he'd lost sight of her after the father-daughter dance.

He'd spent the rest of the reception looking for her, checking his phone every so often. She didn't have the same phobias as he did when it came to weddings, but her sentiments about marriage in general could have been triggered at some point throughout.

He turned on his phone that he'd turned off when he arrived back to his penthouse the night before and went to plug it in, seeing several notifications from texts and voice-mails. The elevator dinged, and Evan stood up, wondering who would be coming up.

When the doors opened, his whole family poured out of it, reminding him of clowns in a clown car.

"Look who's alive. We were worried about you, buddy."

Darren stepped forward and slapped Evan on the back, causing Evan to wince.

"Why? I survived all the events of the wedding and reception. I think I deserve some kind of medal." Evan grinned, rubbing the back of his neck with his hand.

His mother smiled and nodded. "We are definitely proud of you for making it through the night."

Aubrey grinned and walked forward, pulling Evan into a hug. "What? He got to take a nap halfway through, and you're proud of him?"

Evan chuckled. "It's not like you did much. I'm sure you were the social butterfly of the family."

"Please. Someone had to talk to people last night. You looked like you'd rather be anywhere but there, and Aiden, well, we know he's not the best at keeping a conversation going." Aubrey leaned in with a grin, even though her voice stayed the same in volume.

"Uh-huh. I'm sure that was your biggest worry." Evan looked around at his family, some of them sprawled out on the couches and others raiding his kitchen. He looked at Darren and asked, "Where are Emma and the kids?"

"Naptime. All four of them are out, and I didn't want to wake them, so I've been hanging out with everyone else. We're heading back to the ranch today, so I figured I'd let them sleep a bit."

Their mother laughed, and the two guys turned to look at her. "Good luck with that. Usually, you want to coordinate naps with when you're traveling so you can have peace and quiet. Believe me, we had to do that a lot with the triplets, or we would have gone crazy."

The others all burst out laughing, and Darren looked as though he'd been hit in the jaw.

He finally shrugged and said, "Emma is the chief on that one. She said they were all ready for naps, so we'll just do what we have to do to finish up here and then head out later."

Their father came up and patted Darren on the shoulder with one hand and Evan with the other. "Good choice, son. Life is just easier when your wife is happy. Let me tell you."

"What was that I heard?" Evan's mother asked from behind them. Evan turned to see a wide grin on her face.

"You're enjoying this, aren't you?" Evan asked her, trying not to laugh.

She nodded. "Oh, yes."

Evan smiled, but there was no enthusiasm behind it. He watched as his parents bantered back and forth, something they had always done to some degree. A canyon opened in Evan's chest, and he wasn't sure what had caused it. Maybe it was the thought that his parents' marriage was something he wanted, and his loneliness was causing him to want it even more?

Sadie popped into his mind, and a deep regret filled him. He was supposed to dance with her at the reception.

Evan dropped his voice to a near whisper. "Did you see where Sadie went last night? She was supposed to dance with me. I've texted and called, but I haven't heard from her."

"I think she's on a flight back to California. She said something about helping out another bride with a venue problem." Aubrey's eyes softened, and she gave him a small smile. "She didn't text you?"

While the words sounded right, something felt off about them. "Why did she leave already? I waited for her all night but didn't see her."

Evan pulled out his phone and didn't see the fist coming as Aubrey punched him right on the collar bone. The pain reverberated through his shoulders and neck. "Ow! What was that for?"

All the eyes in the room turned to look at the two of

them, and their mother finally spoke. "What's going on between you two? You still need to fight even after all these years?"

"I was just asking where Sadie is, and she pulled out the fist, Mom." Evan tried to do the puppy dog eyes he'd done for years to sway her opinion, but it appeared to have worn off, because his mother didn't crack. He scrolled through his texts, seeing one with Sadie's name a few messages down. He swiped and saw, *Corn Dogs.*

What could be wrong? Was she hurt?

"Well, the girl loves you, and you should have put in more effort to find her. She wouldn't tell me what was wrong, but I assume you have some part in it. Did you say something to make her mad? You must have pushed her away somehow." His mother's words caused him to wince both physically and on the inside.

Throwing his hands up into the air, he said, "I was there. She told me she had to check on some things but she would be there for a few dances."

"How are you going to fix it, though?" Aiden's eyes were boring into Evan's.

"I'm not discussing my love life with my entire family sitting here. That's weird, you know." Not one of them cracked a smile, and the air in the room made him gulp a few times, trying to get enough in to fill his lungs.

"Why not? We've all been here since long before Stacey. We're the best sounding board you're going to get." Aiden raised an eyebrow as he smirked, and Evan knew there was no way he was getting out of this situation without some of his raw feelings coming to the surface.

Raising both hands, Evan chuckled. "I hope you don't think this is an intervention. Because I can handle this on my own. I've been able to correct a lot of things in my life, and most things I've done right the first time. I need to find out how she feels about me." He stood, his heart pounding in his chest.

"Well, do you like her or not?" Aubrey asked, her voice impatient.

"Yeah, I like her. She's funny, smart, and puts me in my place, even if I'm not always happy about that." Evan stared at the design on the carpet under his feet, knowing he'd fallen for a girl he'd known since grade school. Was it possible to love someone after such a short time? As he thought about Sadie and the idea of her two states away, a hole opened up and panic set in. "I'm pretty sure I love her."

Darren walked over and sat on the coffee table in front of Evan. "You've been able to correct almost everything in your life. But your wedding is what you keep to motivate you. Let it go. Start fresh with Sadie. Maybe that will turn into the correction you need to trump your past failure."

"Geez, thanks, Darren."

"Hey, I'm just trying to help you be happy. There's a lot to be said about the love of a good woman."

Swallowing a mound that had formed in his throat, Evan's stomach sank. "That would be hard since she never wants to get married."

Aubrey grinned. "Never say never. She was already coming around to the idea. I could tell that this wedding did more to help change her mindset than anything I've ever seen."

He studied his sister's eyes, waiting for the deception to shine through. But her eyes told him the truth. A surge of adrenaline rushed through him, the kind he'd felt before every big game he'd ever played. Just like those times, he didn't know how it would all play out, but he was ready to go all in.

Grabbing his wallet and his phone, he dialed George. "Hey, George. I'm going to need a ride to the airport ASAP."

Hanging up the phone, he pushed the button to the elevator.

"Good luck, Ev." Aiden grinned at him, leaning against the wall.

"Thanks, A. If this works, we'll have to work on finding you a girl."

"Ha. I may look like you, but the similarities don't extend much further."

"Wait, we need to go down too," Aubrey said, sticking her arm through the opening right before the door closed all the way. The family got off on their own floor, wishing him well.

Evan was grateful for the moments of silence as the elevator continued down to the garage. Walking into the semi-darkness of the underground parking area, he found George waiting for him with the limo.

"Paul is getting the plane ready, sir. You should be ready for takeoff when we arrive."

"That's great, George." He slipped into the back and sat back.

As they arrived at his hangar and before George could get out, Evan jumped out and said, "No worries, George. Take the rest of the day off and hang out with your family. I hope this trip will make me just as happy as you are."

The man grinned, and Evan jumped out, knowing he was going to have to hurry. He didn't want to lose Sadie, and every minute seemed precious now that he knew he wanted to be with her for the rest of his life.

CHAPTER 29

Sadie had been able to curb her emotions until the minute she stepped through the door of her apartment. With the silence that seemed like a fog inside, she couldn't keep the tears from falling again, knowing she should be focusing on the next aspect of her wedding planning business and not the man she'd left in Vegas.

She'd spent most of her dating life comparing men to Evan, and of course, they never seemed to measure up. Now she needed to get over him, to realize he wouldn't want to marry her—or have anything to do with marriage—because her flaws and family life seemed so far off of what he'd grown up with. She didn't know anything about having a strong marriage and family.

If there was one good thing that had come from planning Taryn's wedding, it was the fact that Sadie wasn't completely opposed to the idea of marriage. Maybe not in the traditional sense with the huge wedding and celebration, but something simple, as a promise of a future. With the relationship Dolores and Carl Pearson had, she knew it was possible to stay together and not have it be a yelling match every other minute. Not that the Pearson's parents didn't argue, but at least they respected one another's opinions enough to keep their marriage and family strong.

She hoped she'd someday be able to make a relationship work. After Evan's reaction to the ceremony and getting a speeding ticket after the rehearsal dinner while running away, he might not ever be ready to marry. And she needed someone who wasn't scared of commitment, someone who would never run from her. Especially when she knew now, more than ever, that she needed someone by her side, a best friend she could consult with and divulge all her feelings to. What would her parents' marriage have been like with if they had just confided in one another instead of fighting?

After several hours of being holed up inside her room, her stomach made sure she knew how hungry it was, and because she hadn't been home in a while, there was nothing quick she could eat, which meant she'd have to go out and get something.

There were a few people out and about, but it wasn't so busy that she couldn't get where she needed to go. Making it to the burger place around the corner, she ate her cheese-burger and fries alone. It felt like a symbol of her life. That she was destined to be alone, even though she now wanted to take back everything she'd ever said against marriage.

After picking up a few groceries at the market next to the diner, she made her way back to her apartment, doing her best to keep her mind from wandering back to the loneliness she felt. It reached so deep and felt so heavy that it was as though a large boulder was sitting on top of her chest, only leaving a small airway for her to breathe.

The elevator was broken again, so she trudged the three floors to her apartment, ready to turn on a movie and sleep the night away, knowing she'd need to finish the last few details on the next wedding in a few weeks.

Rounding the staircase, she found the key to her door and looked up, jumping as she saw Evan leaning against the wall next to her door, wearing his now-rumpled wedding attire from the night before.

Trying to regain her composure, she moved forward, focusing the key into the lock and opening the door.

She opened her mouth to say something but found none of the words formed a coherent sentence. Sticking her key into the lock, she turned it and entered the apartment. She dropped the bags on the table and turned to face him.

Evan stood a foot away, and he reached out one hand and rubbed it up and down her arm. "We missed our dance."

"I'm sorry. But I saw your sister and dad dancing together, and something inside me broke, like a tidal wave of my past drowning me. As scary as it is, I want to get married, and I figured with all the emotions you'd gone through during the preparation and execution of the wedding, that asking that of you, if you had feelings for me, would be a stretch."

With his other hand, he lifted a bouquet of daffodils from behind his back. "I came here to tell you I'm sorry for the last two weeks. I know I've been all over the place, physically, mentally, you name it. But I want to say that the past six weeks have opened my eyes to the fact that I love you, Sadie. I love how passionate you are about your work and that you can call me out on my faults. But what I love the most is that you know me. You've seen me fail and didn't treat me any different. You were there for every moment that I needed strength or comfort, and I want to spend the rest of my life with you."

Sadie reached her hand up to her chest, trying to catch her breath. "Did you just say you love me?"

Evan chuckled. "Yeah, I do. I know it's sudden, and if you don't love me—"

"I love you too." Tingles flowed through her body as if in confirmation of her words.

The look on Evan's face was of pure happiness, and in two steps, he'd gathered her up in his arms, pressing his lips to hers with a softness that made her legs go weak. His pulled her closer, deepening the kiss.

After kissing for several seconds, Sadie pulled back, gulping in the air around her. She leaned her forehead against his, relishing the fact that she was actually kissing Evan Pearson, her high school crush, and that he loved her.

"What happens now?" she managed to say, her breathing becoming more even.

Evan took her hand, interlacing her fingers with his. "I'm not sure. But for once, that's okay. I'd like to marry you some day, but only when you're ready. As long as I have you, I'll be the happiest man alive."

After spending most of December working to finish up the last wedding Sadie had for the year, she and Evan took a trip to the ranch for Christmas, where he proposed to her. It might have been quick for many other couples, but with their history, it seemed fitting that it happened around family.

As they drove back to Vegas two days after New Year's, Sadie sat in the passenger seat, admiring the simple solitaire diamond.

"What if we eloped?" She looked over at him, admiring the scruff on his face as he hadn't shaved since they'd arrived at the ranch.

He looked at her, a mischievous grin on his face. "Elope? Are you sure you'd want to do that?"

Sadie shrugged. "I plan weddings for a living. You are deathly afraid of all of the decisions that go into a wedding. It sounds like a great plan to me." She grinned as he scrunched his nose.

"That was the old Evan. As long as you don't leave me at the altar, I'm up for whatever you want to do," he said, glancing at her before turning back to watch the road.

"I'm just saying it might be better for the two of us. We've both had these fears about getting married. What if we just rip off the Band-Aid and do it?"

Evan steered the SUV through traffic and said, "Are you sure you're ready to marry me? Because we've only been dating, like, what? Six weeks?"

"Sounds about right."

"I think I know of a place we could get married today."

Sadie reached over and punched him in the arm. "We are not getting married in a little chapel with an Elvis impersonator. I know there are plenty of people who don't mind that, but I need a bit of a different story if I'm going to survive as a wedding planner."

"How about this weekend? We'll get the license and find a quiet place and go from there."

"Done. I think that was easier than you trying to pick out appetizers for your sister's wedding."

Evan reached over the center console and interlaced her fingers with his, just like he did as often as possible. It was as though just that act alone assured him she wasn't going anywhere. "You're probably right."

* * *

THE NEXT FEW days passed quickly, and Evan was more excited than he thought he'd be at the thought of another wedding. He'd gone all out on the arrangements, making sure to notify the IBC that their retreat to Bermuda was going to be a little more exciting than just a reunion.

He'd brought Aubrey in to help Sadie find a suitable wedding dress from one of the shops under his hotel, telling her that there was no budget on this, and he was excited to see what she'd picked. He was excited just to have her by his side as they pledged their lives to each other.

It had taken some doing to keep the secret of their destination from Sadie, but when he'd picked her up and blindfolded her, he had to laugh as she asked question after question about what was happening.

"Why are we going on an airplane?" she asked once they were on board and ready for takeoff.

"It's a surprise," he said, unable to wipe the wide grin off his face. He took off the blindfold when they were airborne, and he just hoped she'd love it as much as he did.

Just over six hours later, the private jet landed, and Sadie looked at him in awe. "Where are we?"

"Bermuda."

The look of shock on her face was pure gold, and he hoped everyone else was in place.

They got into a car and drove a ways, right up to the sandy beach with the clear light-blue water stretching out before them. He ushered her over to the small building and handed the woman there the bag holding the wedding dress.

"Get changed. I'll meet you out here."

He changed on the other side of the building, donning a white shirt and a pair of khakis, his feet bare as they'd be walking through the sand.

A group text came through, and all it said was, *We're ready.*

Evan's heart raced, hoping Sadie would be okay with his planning. She was the planner after all, but he figured she could use a break on her own wedding. Since it would take place outdoors on the beach, there were only a few flowers and then the few rows of their immediate family and friends.

His father would meet up with Sadie after she'd changed into her gown, allowing her a father-like figure to walk her down the short aisle. He moved into place just as the rest of the group took their seats. All nine of his IBC brothers were there, his family—minus Darren's kids—and Sadie's younger sister, Natasha. It had taken some investigative work to track her down without Sadie knowing, but he at least wanted her sister there to represent the Gibson family since their parents could not.

Aubrey approached him, using her fingers to comb his hair to the side. She even went so far as to lick her thumb and wipe something on his cheek.

Evan chuckled, the nerves getting to him. "We need to find you a guy. You're already way too much like Mom."

"That's not always a bad thing." She turned and moved to sit on the front row in front of his frat brothers.

Evan saw his father first, dressed in a simple suit. Holding onto his arm was Evan's bride. Sadie was dressed in a simple lace dress with a short veil pinned into her curls. As his father escorted her up to him, Evan fought tears.

Once Sadie stood next to him, Evan's father took a seat by his wife. Turning to Sadie, Evan pulled back the veil and saw tears in her eyes as well.

"You planned all this?" she asked in a loud whisper, her hand waving at the rows of chairs. "I can't believe you brought my sister here." The elation on her face eased his fears, and he couldn't believe that today he would be marrying his best friend.

"I figured I you deserved a more elaborate elopement. Besides, I didn't want to just do something in Vegas. I wanted this to be the beginning of our travels together."

Her smile made his pulse jump as the minister began. He turned to the officiator, ready to take this next step.

"Evan Pearson, do you take Sadie Gibson to be your lawful wedded wife—"

"Yes." Evan said it with a grin, never breaking eye contact with the beauty in front of him.

"Sadie Gibson, do you take Evan Pearson—"

"Yes." She smiled.

Evan barely heard the man say the words "husband and wife" before he pulled her to him. Brushing his lips against hers, he paused a second before sealing it with a deeper kiss. He was finally married to his sister's best friend—his best friend—and that kiss held the promise of the future, a future where he had her by his side.

* * *

Keep reading for a sneak peak of Aubrey & Gabe's story in
The Italian Billionaire

* * *

Thank you for reading *Love, Austen!* If you enjoyed it, I would love to see a review from you. You can also subscribe to Britney's newsletter here:
Subscribe to Britney's List

Gabe Alessandro stepped off his private jet and onto the runway of the small airport just outside of Cedar City, Utah. He'd been looking forward to this trip for weeks now, ever since his fraternity brother, Evan Pearson, had told him the reunion of their billionaire club of frat brothers was set to meet at his family ranch some fifty minutes away from this southern town. It meant a break from the constant grind of working at the family eyewear company, Cristallo.

He'd been traveling since four in the afternoon the day before and had to check his watch a few times to see if it had finally changed time zones from Venice, Italy. After a long stop in New York to refuel and sleep, he'd made the quick four-and-a-half-hour flight to Utah.

It had taken him some time to earn his pilot license, but as expensive as it had been, he enjoyed flying, and the flexibility couldn't be beat. The only downside was making sure he had a car waiting for him or at least a rental place nearby so he could get to where he needed to go.

Unloading his suitcase from the plane, he looked around

for signs for where to rent a car. It didn't take long, as the rental cars were set up at the end of the hangars.

"Name and identification?" the agent at the desk asked. She took Gabe's passport and started punching keys on the keyboard, looking as though she'd rather be anywhere than there. After a few minutes, she looked up and said, "What type of car would you like?"

Leaning forward on the counter, Gabe smiled wide and paused a moment to see if she'd break out of her foul mood. When she raised her eyebrows, he said, "Do you have any convertibles?"

The woman turned her attention back to the screen and then said, "We have one available. But it's yellow." She looked at him, doubt clouding her features.

"Even better. I'll take it."

With her eyebrows pinching together, she said, "You do know that it's supposed to snow tonight, right? You're sure you want to take a convertible on the roads?"

"Is that a bad thing?" Gabe tried to think of his few experiences with snow in Italy. He'd never had to think about getting a different car because of it. Most of the snow was in the northern provinces, near the ski resorts. And it had been a while since he'd visited any of those.

The woman tilted her head down and gave him a fake smile. "You might want an SUV to make sure you don't get stuck anywhere. Where is your destination?"

"Aspen Hollow."

Nodding, the woman said, "Okay, I have several crossover vehicles that I recommend for traveling there. You'll be going through some passes, and the storm is supposed to be worse later tonight." She compiled all the receipts and paperwork into a small folder and handed it to him. "Just go out this door and to the left, and you'll see signs to our lot. Just choose anything from row C. Have a nice day."

"You too." Gabe nodded and walked in the direction she'd pointed. He felt sorry for her. No one should hate their job that much. Then again, he'd been hoping this trip would rejuvenate his enthusiasm for eyewear. He'd been working so much the past few years that he'd hardly had time off to enjoy himself. At thirty, he felt as if he'd worked enough to be nearly forty already.

He made it to the row of cars in the parking garage, but none of them were what he would've picked. He'd just have to survive a week in Aspen Hollow with what he considered an elderly car. Picking the brightest red SUV they had on the lot, he loaded his suitcase and hopped in. His phone buzzed as he turned the ignition, and he smiled when he saw Evan's name.

"Pearson. I just made it to Cedar City."

"Awesome. Sam's plane just landed, and he should be at baggage claim soon. Will you give him a ride?"

"Sure thing. They said I shouldn't get a convertible, so I've got loads of room." Gabe turned around and surveyed the interior. This would be nice for a family. The thought of it brought memories of Nicoletta to the surface, and he did his best to push them away. But the ache for someone at his side and children he could cheer on in sports and other activities settled just inside his chest, reminding him that even though he had his parents and sister in his life, he was still alone.

Evan's chuckle carried through the phone, pulling him back to the present. "Yeah, we're supposed to get hit with a storm tonight, so be careful but hurry."

Gabe ended the call and watched the signs for the exit. After showing the attendant his paperwork, he pulled out of the garage and followed the signs to the commercial side of the airport.

Sam Gutierrez was another frat brother, coming from Argentina. Other than a quick conversation at their other club members' weddings, it had been quite a while since they'd spent much time together. Especially since he hadn't been able to make it to the funeral of their Delta Phi mentor, Dan Montgomery, the year before, when the club had taken a few days to be together in his memory.

Sam was waiting next to the curb with a suitcase and what looked like a laptop bag.

"You made it," Gabe said. He parked and got out of the car. Striding up to his friend, the two of them clapped each other on the back.

"Barely. I got sandwiched between two large people on the last flight, and the air broke. It was longer than I wanted; that's for sure." Sam grinned, his dark brown hair sprinkled with gray catching the dim light from the sky. Of all the frat brothers, he was the oldest by only a few months, but it had been a while since Gabe had really looked at him, and he seemed like he'd aged at least five years.

Gabe reached up and rubbed at it. "What happened to you, old man? When did you start going gray?"

"Since the year after graduation. My father was completely white by this point, so I guess I should be grateful I don't look decades older already."

After placing his luggage in the back, Gabe plugged the address for the Pearson Ranch into his phone, and they headed out.

"Are you ready to be with all the guys?" Gabe asked, watching the road as it wound around to the exit of the airport.

"Yes, I'm definitely ready for this trip. Business has been busier than ever, and I feel like I'm maxed out." Sam leaned his head back against the headrest, breathing out a deep sigh.

With a quick nod, Gabe said, "I'm feeling a little burned out myself. But you work in the energy business. I'd think you'd have plenty of that lying around." He chuckled.

Sam gave him a mock laugh. "If only that was how it worked."

Gabe didn't press for an explanation. He'd read enough in the papers about the fights over energy resources in South America, and he just hoped the stress wouldn't send his friend to the hospital for health problems like it had Sam's father…or Gabe's father, for that matter.

"I'm glad to hear it's not just me needing the break," Sam said as he stared out the window. "Now if we can just avoid all the married guys trying to set us up with women, it will be the perfect getaway."

Gabe listened to the voice on his phone giving him directions as he thought about Sam's words. As much as he wanted it to be a joke, four of their frat brothers were already settling down, and as much as Gabe told himself it wasn't a competition, part of him felt like he was going to end up last in the race.

But he didn't have time for a girlfriend right now, nor would it be practical to look for one while he was in the States. From everything he'd learned in college about American girls, as much as they talked about dating foreign guys, he'd rarely seen them actually living in Italy. He could understand that. His family was a big part of his life, one of the reasons he worked so hard, and it would be hard to live far away from them for longer than a year at a time.

"We'll stick together on that one." Gabe reached out his fist, and Sam bumped his against it. Sadness filled Gabe, but he pushed it away. He wasn't going to ruin this trip by worrying about his single status.

To keep reading, check out *The Italian Billionaire.*

<u>Love Austen Series</u>

Love, Austen

Austen, Party of Two

Austen Unscripted

Matched, Austen

<u>International Billionaire Club</u>

The Australian Billionaire

The French Billionaire

The British Billionaire

The Vegas Billionaire

The Italian Billionaire

<u>Christmas at Coldwater Creek</u>

Love in a Blizzard

Love in the Lights

Love in a Snapshot

Love in the Details

Subscribe to the newsletter to get updates on books coming out, cover reveals and the opportunity for giveaways!

ABOUT THE AUTHOR

Britney Mills was born in Utah but parts of her heart lie in Boston, Washington D.C. and Germany. Her love of writing began with the third grade book her teacher assigned her to write and she spent hours hidden behind her mother's couch writing pages and pages about knights and castles. Now she writes about romance. Go figure.

When she's not mothering her four small children, writing or reading, she's probably out playing a sport, going on a hike, or binge watching a murder mystery series. The way to her heart is through homemade chocolate chip cookies and five minutes peace.

ACKNOWLEDGMENTS

Thank you so much for reading this book! I hope you enjoyed it and make sure to leave a review!

You, the reader, are the one I think about as I work through these novels and thank you for continuing to support me. Starting a new series gets a little scary because it's new and I just hope you love these characters as much as I have.

Thank you, Max, for taking the kids every Thursday so I can pour my heart out on the page. I'm a better mother and a more sane wife when I have those small breaks.

Julie L. Spencer, Elizabeth McCay, Shannon Symonds and Deborah Goodman. Some of the best and funnest romance people I could associate with. I love our Thursday night chats and the late hours talking about whatever is going on in our lives. The long Facebook threads and the fun laughter as we work through our bad first drafts down to the final edits.

To Christina Schrunk for her patience in working with me on these books. Her ideas and insight help to spark those last final puzzle pieces to help the book come together and I am so grateful for her.

To Krista Burdine for proofreading this book. She keeps me sane so I don't have to reread the book 100 times before publishing to hopefully get all of the errors out.

To Blue Valley Author Services, AKA Victorine Lieske and her awesome sister for making the cover. Especially for the last minute change of the guys eyes.

If you want news on when the next book comes out or my progress on the series, make sure to subscribe to the list so you don't miss anything.

We are grateful for readers like you and can't wait for you to enjoy the next book!